# FINDING
*you*

international bestselling author

# S.K. HARTLEY

Vicky,

Stay awesome!!

♡ SK Hartley

Editing: Ultra Editing Co.
Interior formatting by Cassy Roop of Pink Ink Designs
https://www.facebook.com/PinkInkDesignsbyCassy

For my mother-in-law, Suzanne.
*Waves*

# FINDING
*you*

*prologue*

T HE SMELL OF ANTISEPTIC and cleanliness was what I remembered most, the burning in the back of your throat and the watering of your eyes as it takes over each one of your senses, reminding you that you are, in fact, very much awake and it wasn't a nightmare.

I stared around the small room for some time, trying to take in everything but I absorbed nothing. The four walls that encased what was left of my family, felt as though they were caving in on me. At the tender age of ten, I was feeling suffocated from the outside in as we waited for the news that we knew was going to come.

My gaze made its way around the room for the twentieth time, landing on my mother whose howling noises caused my skin to prickle and my heart to race. She'd been inconsolable since the call arrived merely hours ago. It was that very sound which alerted me to her breaking heart, the sound so prominent,

I was sure it shook my very core. Racing down the staircase, I found my mother screaming and howling hysterically, drowning out the regular noise of the cartoon show from the TV we'd left on. I stared in shock at my mother as she clutched at her chest, as though her heart was being ripped from her body, powerless to stop the crushing pain which seeped within. Tears fell from her beautiful blue eyes, blurring her usually flawless, made-up face.

I didn't recognize my own mother as the pain and agony shredded through her heart. On the deep blue carpet of our hallway, my mother was sprawled on the floor, a tangled mess next to the phone which was clawed from the wall in a moment of absolute panic and distress.

Her voice broke through the sound of her wails, it was croaky and barely audible from the harsh rise and fall from her chest as she heaved from the devastating words which were trying to escape her mouth, but nothing filtered through.

Getting down on the floor, I did the only thing I could think of, I comforted her as best as a young ten-year-old could in that situation.

My older brother, Tate, and his best friend, Logan, quickly came down to see what was going on. My gaze lifted from my mother, who was holding onto me with so much force, I could barely breathe, and stared at my brother and his best friend. I had no idea what was going on and I wish I'd never found out.

Logan took one look at the scene laid out before him and ran out of the door to his house next door. Within seconds, he and his mother were by our sides, pulling me from my mother's grasp and taking her into the living room to sit down on our worn sofa. I stood there wide-eyed as Mrs. White tended to my mother, trying to find out what happened. Then, a simple sentence broke my world.

"Brandon's been in a car wreck. We need to go to the hospital."

I could feel my world tilting on its axis as the words did something I couldn't describe. It felt as though my chest was splitting down the center, the pain bouncing off my chest cavity and resonating deep within me.

The next thirty minutes were a whirlwind of getting into Mrs. White's car as she pulled away from our small home, taking us towards the hospital to locate my father. Tears fell from my eyes but no sound came from my lips as I stared out into the darkness of the evening, until we suddenly came to a screeching halt.

I held my breath as the force of the car threw me back into my seat. My hand instantly went out to my left, latching onto Logan's. His hand squeezed mine and a little part of me started to feel safe within the chaos. Tate was sitting on the opposite side to Logan in the car, his hand visible on the window beside him. I looked over at my brother, trying to get some sort of indication as to what was going on and why we had suddenly come to a halt when my mother's screams broke the silence of the car.

My gaze moved to the front of the car, locking onto the scene that lay before us and that's when I knew, I'd never be the same again. My hands moved before I could register what I was doing. Unbuckling my belt, I threw myself out of the car and to the scene that displayed absolute devastation. Blue and red lights flickered around me, the noise of the night eerily silent as my feet took me to a living nightmare. Right there, in front of my eyes, was my father's truck. Screaming broke the sound barrier, piercing my ears at an alarming rate. I threw my hands over my ears as I ran towards my father's truck, only to be stopped mid-stride with large arms wrapping around my mid-section.

"It's okay, darling." A gruff, male voice said, his voice distorted from my hands covering my ears.

Out of reflex, I pulled away my hands, instantly replacing them as the screaming continued. Then I realized, the screaming was coming from me. Shaking my head and wiggling my small frame, I tried to release myself from the strangers hold. I could feel the cold metal of his badge digging into my skin between my shoulder blades, indicating he was a cop. Flailing my legs, my foot hit something hard and before I knew it, I was running back towards the truck.

The screaming stopped the moment I saw the absolute destruction before me. My father's truck was completely mangled in a way that looked completely unnatural, metal was twisted and crushed like a concertina and I struggled to recognize particular parts of the truck, fluid leaked from the mass of metal and glass crunched under foot as I took another step forward. I could hear yelling and screaming in the faded background but I pushed it aside, only concentrating on the thundering sound of my heartbeat as blood flowed around my body at a faster pace.

I could feel the hot, wet tears streaking my face the moment I took the last step towards the truck, trying to work out what happened. Then, everything became visible. Surrounding the truck were paramedics, firefighters and cops, all trying to lift the roof of the truck - not one of them noticing me as they concentrated on the task at hand. My eyes roamed the scene before me, noticing another paramedic, but this one was in the back of the truck, holding onto something in the front…

My father's head.

There in the front seat of the truck was my father - his body covered in a deep red hue as his eyes fluttered open before closing again. Through all the chaos, I heard the sound of dripping. Wondering where the irritating noise was coming from, I looked towards my feet, my gaze locking onto more of the red fluid which looked to be dripping from the door of the truck.

I was standing in my father's blood.

The screaming started again, the hoarse cry of my own pain breaking through the barrier and alerting the team of people to my presence. I could see one of the cops moving around the mess to come to my side but in a last ditch attempt to help myself understand that this wasn't a nightmare, my hands dived into what was the window of the truck.

My hands instinctively went to his face, my soft, warm touch a stark difference to his wet and cold skin as the blood coated my fingertips. I pulled back my hands, not truly understanding what was going on. Turning on my heel, I came face to face with my brother's best friend, Logan. Unable to control my own body's reaction, I fell straight into his arms as he pulled me away from the ugly scene.

The next thing I knew, we were back in the cold, white room. My gaze was still focused on my mother as she cried into Mrs. White's neck, trying to pull comfort from one of her closest friends. Mrs. White stole glances at us kids, trying to piece together whether we were okay but I was far from it. The blood still coated my fingers and the lump, I was unable to swallow, remained lodged in my throat.

No longer able to take in my mother's heartbreak, my gaze moved and seemed to focus on the back wall. A mass of painted daisies adorned the wall, each one a little different from the other, just like us. Each daisy consisted of ten white petals and one yellow center. I smiled a little, it gave me comfort to focus on something that was so delicate, yet strong. Slowly, I started counting the daisies in my head, trying to soothe my rapid heartbeat.

One...

Two...

Three...

With my eyes still focused on the wall, I backed up to the worn blue sofa. My arm grazed the fabric and I noticed scratches and pieces missing from the piece of furniture. There was history in that sofa, a history of other broken families waiting for news or comfort. It was unmistakable, the horror and pain the sofa had seen over the years it had been sat there. I could feel it seep into my bones the longer I sat.

Four...

Five...

Six...

My attention was suddenly pulled away from my daisy counting, drawn to a man wearing a white coat. He walked through the door of the small, white room, the pained expression on his face evident as he took a seat beside my mother and turned to her. My counting had soon ceased, my attention solely on the man whose pain for us dripped from him in waves. The words that poured from his mouth had me frozen in an instant, unable to take in exactly what he was saying. Everything was a blur.

*Car crash.*

*Drunk driver.*

*Revived at the scene.*

The words replayed over and over in my mind as I tried to understand what was unfolding before me, but my mind was in a haze of utter confusion. The only thing that truly made sense to me in that moment was to be with my father.

So, I ran.

I ran from the room, running until my lungs burned and my eyes stung with unshed tears, trying desperately to find the only man who I promised to love, the man who'd kissed the cuts and scrapes better, the man who taught me how to ride a bike. My daddy.

"Daddy!" I screamed, hoping I would hear his voice, hoping that this was just one long nightmare.

I was quickly becoming frantic, the corridor I found myself in seeming like it would never end. There were so many doors, so many rooms and adjoining corridors and I didn't know which direction to take. I remembered what my father had said to me when we camped last year, "If you're lost, walk north. You'll always find your way if you walk north." So I did. Thinking back, it was such an insignificant thing at the time but gave me so much comfort. Ignoring the curious looks from other people, I looked into every room down the long, narrow corridor that housed endless patient rooms. The more I looked, the more I became frustrated. I just wanted to get to my father.

Suddenly, I stopped dead in my tracks as I ran past a room with its door open. I didn't know what it was that stopped me, but when I stepped into the doorway I found I couldn't take my eyes off the man lying on the bed. His eyes were so many shades of blue; I could've easily got lost trying to count the different hues. The more I stared, the more I noticed tiny gold flecks entwined around the deeper shades of blue, causing his eyes to pop with so much more intensity. Although his eyes were captivating, nothing could prepare me for the haunted look that covered the poor man's face.

The intensity of his pain vibrated through me, his appearance only showcasing the distress and trauma he'd clearly been through. I couldn't look away. As I took a step forward, the stranger closed his eyes and turned his face away from me. It was enough to snap me back into the present and find my father.

With my fear escalating, I started running again, frantically checking every room and wondering if I was ever going to find him. Finally, I made it to the last door in the corridor. A deep sigh escaped my lips when I saw his name written on a white board outside the room.

It was the silence I noticed first, it was hauntingly unsettling, sky rocketing my fear to its peak. Swallowing hard, I tried to suppress the ungodly urge to vomit when I walked into the room, my eyes quickly landing on my father. This was the man who had shielded me since I was first placed into his arm as an innocent child. I gasped, he didn't look like the man I had seen hundreds of times before; he looked broken, damaged.

As my eyes adjusted to the harsh lighting of the room, I noticed my father's eyes had swollen shut. The darkest of bruises lined the skin beneath his eyes and dried blood stuck to matted hair which lay over a fresh white bandage. I tentatively made my way towards him, wanting so desperately to hold his hand, to place a kiss on his cheek like I always did, but the potent smell of car fumes penetrated my nostrils as my eyes took in the hellish nightmare before me.

"Daddy?" I whimpered, convinced he was fast asleep.

There was no answer, of course there was no answer but I was determined not to believe the events of the day had truly happened. Now closer, his injuries became more apparent. Some of his right ear was torn at the lobe and deep scratches adorned his once beautiful face, but it was the unseen injuries that caused the most damage. I later found out the force of the impact caused irreversible damaged and he would never wake from his slumber.

I was frozen with fear, the realization that I may never see or speak to my father again, hitting me at full force. It was enough to encourage me to move to his bedside and attempt to hold his hand. With my whole body trembling, I gently placed my tiny hand in his, my tear filled eyes watching and waiting for any sign of movement, of life.

It was something I would always remember; his once warm, welcoming hands were cold and pale.

As I squeezed his hand I finally noticed the tubes and wires scattered all around us. Machines beeped, numbers flashed and the smell of car fumes only got stronger. Then, the beeping and flashing suddenly became erratic. Different colored lines and more numbers I didn't understand, appeared on the screen.

What was happening?

Why wasn't he waking up?

Why...why?

Fear, devastation and pain like I'd never felt crashed through me like a tsunami, with each crash of the waves only causing my lungs to burn and my heart to pound viciously. It was becoming harder and harder to breathe with every passing second. With my throat restricted and burning like a wild fire, I screamed out in emotional and physical pain of what lay before me.

"Daddy! Wake up. You have to wake up, daddy. Please, please don't leave me." I cried in a hoarse whisper but he didn't move nor did he try and comfort me. He lay there, still and lifeless. "Daddy please, I promise to do my homework and stop arguing with Tate and, and I will…I will. Please, I need you, daddy!"

I not only pleaded with my father that day, but also God, yet he still didn't move.

Scrambling, I quickly tried to climb onto the bed where he lay, wanting to place my head on his chest like I always did when I was upset. I wanted him to kiss the top of my head and tell me everything was going to be okay. I wanted my daddy back.

I was quickly aware of voices around me. People were screaming and crying, drowning out the machines that were carefully positioned around my father's bed. Arms swiftly wrapped around my stomach, pulling me away from the safe cover of my father's chest and little part of me was destroyed.

"No!" I screamed in protest, trying to hold on to my father's lifeless hand as I was being pulled away. "Let me go!" I screamed between gut wrenching sobs.

They didn't let me go.

They tore me away from my father, comforting me, telling me it was okay. It wasn't okay, nothing was okay. I wanted my father.

I could hear the harrowing sounds of people crying, the hushed whispers just as loud as the sobs. Although louder than usual, I couldn't make out what they were saying, it had all become white noise. The thundering of my heart beating heavily against my chest caught my attention, the feeling of my heart wanting to break free of the confines of its cavity - it was so loud, so brutal, and so painful.

Suddenly, a voice pulled me away from the aching feeling in my chest. The voice was so clear, so crisp that it splintered through my pain, through the thundering noises around me, shutting everything else out.

"Turn off the life support."

It was all I heard, all I needed to hear. My father was never coming back, they were just going to let him go. Even as a young and innocent child, I understood.

Warm arms embraced me, pulling me into a hug that took my breath away. The next thing I remember, I was back at home rousing in and out of sleep. Within my sleepy haze, I noticed Logan crouched down on the floor beside me, wearing a pained expression as he stroked lazy circles onto the skin of my forearm.

"I will always protect you, Neva." He whispered as my eyes locked on my fingers, the blood was no longer there but very much imprinted in my skin for a lifetime.

My innocence was stolen from me that day, an innocence I would never get back. My life would forever be changed because of one single event, an event that would impact anything and everyone around me, including everyone I held dear.

You think you know my story. A story of heartbreak, a story of weakness, one without strength. But this isn't just a story, this is my life, my past, present and future colliding and destroying everything in its path.

Welcome to my hell.

*one*

TEN WHITE PETALS.
One yellow center.
One…
Two…
Three…
I could feel the hands around my throat, my breathing becoming shallow as I tried to scream on the inside, not knowing if my nightmare, filled with the demons of my past, would kill me while I slept. My heartbeat roared as it pounded relentlessly against my chest, leaving a ringing sensation in my ears. The smell of antiseptic suddenly hit me, the burning scent shocking my senses. The scent was so potent, so strong that I could taste it in the back of my throat – thick and heavy. The pressure around my neck loosened enough for me to get my bearings. I was back at the bridge again, pinned to the cold, hard asphalt by someone,

or something, I couldn't see nor describe. There was nowhere to go, there was never anywhere to go. I was trapped on the bridge that led to nowhere, keeping me forever in the darkness, never to see the light again.

I could taste the fear drowning out the antiseptic deep in my throat, my fear pouring into my gut as my body absorbed it. It was in my bones, in my soul, gripping me with pure terror. My eyes became transfixed as I stared up at the demon above me, a black and smoky silhouetted figure towering over my tiny frame. I've never been able to make out who or what the demon was, but it was always there, always haunting, always causing pain.

The grip around my neck tightened once more, my hands reaching out either side of me as I tried to reach for anything to help free me, but there was nothing, there was always nothing. I could see the bridge clearly but somehow never really feel it against my skin, just the subconscious pressure against my back as if I was floating. Endlessly floating.

"Stop. Please, no!"

I wanted to scream, wanted to cry out but my vision was becoming blurry as my head swam with weightlessness. Images projected against the dark shadow of the demon above me, a car severely damaged, flashing blue lights and the screaming I could never run away from - absolute chaos.

The demon squeezed a little harder and I was sure I was about to die. I was ready to let go, to follow through with the weightlessness that took over every part of my being, but I never died in my nightmares. I hung on the edge, the demon forcing me to remember, forcing me to see the destruction I couldn't seem to let go of.

Without warning, the nightmare slowly started to release me, the twisted dark depths of my past slowly fading into a painful reminder of what was cruelly taken. What I'll never get back.

The sound of my heartbeat was the first thing alerting me to my surroundings. My lids were heavy, so heavy I didn't think I could physically open my eyes.

"Come back to me."

A familiar soothing voice wrapped around my mind, trying to release me of my own painful imprisonment.

I desperately tried to speak to the voice, wanting it to pull me out from the torture that held me captive within my own mind. My tongue was heavy and my mouth dry as I clicked it against the back of my teeth. A fine sheen of sweat took over my skin as my toes curled in pain, my heart becoming heavy with unrelenting sadness.

The light was almost too much to bear as I finally managed to open my eyes, squinting as the light penetrated hard, burning right through me. There was a figure above me once more, but this time it wasn't dark and twisted like the demons in my nightmares, it was home. I was home.

"You haven't had a nightmare in a really long time."

I squinted my eyes painfully as I tried to adjust to the light, the darkness of my nightmare had concealed me for too long, keeping me under and not letting go. The voice soothed my soul and punctured through the dark depths of my mind, clearing the haze of dark clouds that rested like an imprint behind my eyes.

"Logan?" I croaked, my voice hoarse and shaky as if the hand that pinned me down caused physical harm. Some people say nightmares can't physically hurt you. Mine did, you just couldn't see the bruises – they were buried deep within. My heart and soul, they were bruised, broken and shattered, my mind tumbling back to places I wouldn't want an enemy to experience.

"I'm here. It's okay, you're safe." He whispered, placing a glass of water in my shaking hands. I licked my painfully dry lips before forcing the water down my parched throat. It relieved the unnatural dryness but not the sour and vile taste. I could still taste the fear laced with antiseptic.

"More." I croaked, holding out the glass like a child. I needed to get rid of the taste, otherwise I was sure I would vomit. My stomach was already turning from the fear which still penetrated deep within. Before I could blink, my empty glass was replaced with another full glass of water. He'd been prepared, he was always prepared.

"Thank you." I whispered, my voice becoming clearer as the water coated my throat. "I'm sorry." I apologized, trying to hide the shame laced within my voice. I hated him seeing me like this, seeing the broken parts of me.

"Don't be sorry for something you have no control over." He said gently, the pad of his thumb wiping tears from my eyes. "Come on, let's get you in the shower."

Nodding my head, I tentatively threw back my sweat soaked sheets and slowly swung my legs off the bed. Logan placed my limp arm around his neck, ready to support my weight. Inhaling, I tried to settle my still pounding heart while pushing through my legs to stand on my feet. On shaky legs, I moved my right foot forward. My entire body felt heavy from the sheer exhaustion from the latest nightmare. Melting into Logan's side, he all but carried me to the en-suite bathroom in my dorm.

The oversized shirt clung to my body as Logan placed me in the shower fully clothed, the water warming my skin, but I knew no matter how hot the stream of water may be, it would never warm my aching heart.

"I'll be right outside the door if you need me, okay?"

I could only nod, my throat constricting as the sobs threatened to escape. On a shaky breath, I pushed away the unshed tears as I mulled over what happened. The demons were back, my past melting into my present. It was the ten-year anniversary of my father's death. The event must've triggered my nightmare, triggered my worst fears. My stomach churned violently, making me nauseous and dizzy. Inhaling slowly, I paused as I waited for the sickening feeling to subside.

I closed my eyes as the minutes passed, praying I stayed up right. Breathing steadily, I peeled myself out of the wet fabric before stepping beneath the spray of water. I took a longer shower than normal, hoping the warmth of the water would wipe away any evidence of the brutal nightmare I'd endured. Ten minutes later, I stepped out, quickly drying myself before brushing my teeth. Turning, I found another oversized checkered shirt hanging on the back of the bathroom door. Shrugging, I threw it on and found some boy shorts in my emergency stash of clean underwear in the hamper before opening the door.

I gasped the moment I came face to face with Logan leaning against the door frame. My eyes racked the entire length of him, staring right at me was six feet two inches of pure male. Long lashes framed the clearest brown eyes and I swore if you looked hard enough, you'd see small scattered flecks of green. His chocolate brown hair was styled into that mussed up and sexy look, sitting at the perfect length to run your fingers through it. I instantly stopped my ministrations with my eyes as I noticed his full, defined pink lips morph into a smirk. How could he look like that every morning?

He wore low-slung jeans designed to show off his toned body, coupled with a white t-shirt, tight enough to count each and every one of his muscles on his sculptured torso. He was my brother's best friend, but even I couldn't deny the hotness that seeped out of his every pore. I suddenly forgot what I was doing, all appropriate thoughts had flown out of the window.

"You okay?" He asked, his brow furrowing slightly.

My mind drew a blank, wasn't I supposed to do something with my brain and my mouth?

I needed to focus.

"I'm fine." My mouth finally engaged with my brain, an involuntary shiver rolling down my spine as Logan eyed my bare legs.

"Hey, so that's where my favorite shirt went!" He said suddenly, shaking his head as if trying to remove thoughts from his mind.

I'd borrowed his shirt a couple of days before. It was deep green in color, matching the flecks in his eyes. I had been over at my brother's dorm watching a movie when I'd spilt soda onto my camisole. My brother had thrown Logan's shirt at me and told me to wear it. It smelled like Logan, a perfect balance of spiced apple and musky cinnamon, reminding me of Christmas. It was my favorite shirt.

"You can't have it, it's mine." I smiled, pulling it closer to my body. But the smile faded when my stomach churned once again, as if my body was reminding me of why Logan was here in the first place. I shouldn't be smiling.

"Do you know how many women would kill for my shirt?" Logan asked cockily as he followed me from the bathroom into my room, standing at the edge of my bed.

"I would kill for you, Logan, but not for your shirt." I said sincerely, a smile gracing my lips.

Logan White was like a brother to Tate. They'd known each other since kindergarten and been inseparable ever since. Tate and Logan were both seniors who shared a dorm room. My best friend, Low, and I were sophomores and shared a dorm room as well. I had met Low in high school, she was the devil on my shoulder that pushed me, sometimes too far but I loved her like the sister I never had.

"Are you going to give me my shirt or am I going to have to take it from you?" He smirked, raising his brow as his eyes twinkled with mischief, causing me to take a step back.

"I don't think..."

He quickly cut me off, lifting me from the floor and slung over his defined shoulder. I let out a scream and started pounding his solid back. Jeez, he had muscles there too?

"Put me down, Logan, or I swear I will castrate you!" I screamed at him.

Suddenly he stopped mid-stride. Turning my head to look at him, his sexy smirk was back on his face once more.

Oh shit, this wasn't good.

"Neva, you know I have an amazing view of your ass right now?" He said, before slapping my right cheek, quickly making me yelp in surprise.

"Ouch!" I yelped before he ever so slowly slid me down the front of his body, ensuring I felt every single tight muscle. Staring straight into my eyes, he slowly caressed my ass with only the thin material separating him from touching my stinging flesh, moving his palm in lazy circles.

I had to bite back a moan from escaping my lips. It felt, well, nice.

"Morning campers! What...oh."

Jerking my head into the direction of my best friend, the look on Low's face brought me back down to reality. Her expression was laced with confusion and amusement. Noticing me, she flashed a wink before taking a sip of her coffee. She must've gotten up early for coffee.

"Morning." Logan replied in a whisper as he hung his head and swiftly left my room.

"Well, THAT was a surprise! What was all that about?" Low asked, stepping into the room and handing me her coffee to drink.

I gingerly took a sip, loving the warmth it brought with the amazing taste.

"Ugh, he's such a man whore!" I sighed, handing her back her coffee. "But enough about me, what the hell are you wearing?!" I took in my best friend's less-than-conservative attire with a smirk.

Low had to be wearing the most revealing damn top I had ever seen, coupled with denim shorts that showed so much of her ass it should be illegal. Looking down her never ending legs, my eyes landed on a pair of pink cowboy boots. Her hair was a natural honey blonde, it was gorgeous, and she had curled it at the ends slightly.

I chuckled at my best friend's outfit, knowing that guys were going to drool the moment they saw her. Today we were both starting our sophomore year of college and I was looking forward to getting back into classes, whereas Low, on the other hand, clearly had different ideas.

"What? I intend on picking up my future husband this year!" She said, waving me off as she walked into the bathroom. I sighed before my stomach churned once more. This was definitely not good.

"And I intend on making sure my best friend isn't mauled by men when they see those shorts!" I pointed to the ridiculous denim on her legs that hid pretty much nothing. "Where do you get those anyway, Baby Gap?"

She rolled her eyes.

"Someone's had a dose of happy this morning." She mocked, sitting on her bed opposite mine and crossing her legs.

I swore if I saw more than I needed because of those shorts, I was going to burn them.

"Just a bad night." I cringed, realizing I probably shouldn't have mentioned the dream to Low, she was protective and it was damn scary.

"A nightmare?" She stood, taking a seat on my bed and patting the duvet next to her. "You haven't had one of those in-"

"A long time, I know." I finished for her.

The nightmares weren't something I could control but then again, who could? They were reminders, pain holders, dream crushers and soul breakers but mine could wake the dead from the terror they inflicted. It had been a long time since my last one, creeping in from time to time when I was caught off guard. I hated them, but most of all, I hated what they represented.

Weakness.

My weakness.

## two

I ROLLED MY EYES AS I watched twenty girls flock around Tate's Jeep the moment I stepped out of the truck. It was the guys' meeting spot. In other words, it was a drool fest full of adoring college girls. It was disgusting watching girls fight over Logan, and I'm sure I just heard Georgia Mathews ask if he wanted a quickie before class, ugh.

"Have fun, man whore." I shouted over my shoulder as I made my way through the throngs of females trying to get their hands on the 'sex god' that was Logan White. My brother just shook his head laughing at the scene around him.

Low chuckled, "Do they all have to be so obvious that they would drop their panties for him with a snap of his fingers?" I rolled my eyes at my best friend. Does she really want to make me gag before my first class?

"Ugh, that's gross Low." I said as we made our way into the building. Spring Water College was quite small compared to state colleges, but it boasted glorious grounds and antique style architecture that made you instantly fall in love with the place. Spring Water was a small coastal town in Mississippi that flaunted majestic beaches and scorching hot weather, but it was known for some awesome college parties, so everyone went to SWC.

"So anyway, I will text you the place to meet me after class okay?" Low said before she pulled me into a fierce hug "See you later." Her smile wasn't her usual megawatt, knock-them-off-your-feet smile. She knew I was still struggling with the hurt I felt every time I walked into my music class.

I was ten when my father was killed. He had been driving to the store on a cold night, a few weeks before Christmas. He had taken a short-cut, which meant driving over the old wooden bridge that crossed into town. Black ice had covered nearly every road in our little town, but it wasn't the cold temperatures or the dangerous road conditions that killed him. It was a drunk driver that hurtled towards him on that bridge, skidding on black ice. Dad was pinned down in the car by the steering column of the truck. It had taken fifteen firemen to get him out before he was transferred to the hospital, where he later died.

Shaking my head, I tried to remember all the fun times that we shared. We were so alike in looks and attitude and shared the same passion for music, but the most vivid memories were the songs he used to sing to me at night before I went to sleep. It's where my love of music came from. Dad had played the guitar and tried to teach me too, but I preferred listening to him play for me.

The day of dad's funeral I locked myself in my room with

his guitar, I was determined to learn how to play it. I found all of dad's old Guitar 101 books and started from scratch, learning each note and each bar until my fingertips were numb. The only people who knew I played were mom, Logan, Tate, and Low, but this year, I wanted other people to understand my passion for music.

Every time I picked up my dad's guitar, I fell in love with music all over again. I understood why my dad loved it so much. I couldn't talk about what happened to my dad. It was just too painful, he was my everything. But the lyrics could tell people for me. The pain and grief I felt when he died has stuck with me ever since.

I was walking towards my class when I heard it, the perfect melody of guitar and voice. A voice so hauntingly hypnotic, a male voice singing a perfect rendition of "I Don't Want to Miss a Thing" by Aerosmith. My legs decided at this particular moment to start moving. Making my way to the room that housed the most beautiful voice I had ever heard, my head pounded as I desperately tried to find the source of the voice.

Pushing my way through the crowded corridor, I was spellbound with this voice, it felt like a knife penetrating straight through me, slicing me in half. Suddenly my legs seemed to stop working, I could hear the voice more clearly. It was so moving, I could feel tears sting my eyes.

Finally prying my eyes away from the ground beneath me, I locked eyes with the person who possessed a voice that could break me, shatter me, and put me back together again. Leaning against the wall was the perfect specimen of a man, large hands caressed his worn guitar as he played note after beautiful note.

But this time, it wasn't the perfect sound of the strum of his guitar capturing me or his voice. It was just him.

Dark lashes rested against perfectly high cheekbones as he sang with his eyes closed, lost in his own moment. His hair, dark as a midnight sky, gently swayed as he bobbed his head in time to the melody. His beautiful lips captivated me as his smooth and sexy voice filled my ears.

Suddenly he looked up, straight at me. I was paralyzed. His eyes were an unbelievable combination of blues that were so intense that I had to quickly look away. I could no longer see or hear the throngs of other students. All I could see, hear, and feel was this man. His voice was so smooth, so sexy, so understanding that I felt compelled to take a seat in front of him but my legs now decided they weren't going to move.

He was still staring straight at me as the lyrics rolled off his tongue, mesmerizing me further.

*"I could stay lost in this moment forever..."*

Shivers penetrated my body, it felt like he was singing just for me, as if I was his own captured audience.

*"Every moment spent with you is a moment I treasure..."*

I had to close my eyes and bite my lip to stop the moan in the back of my throat escaping from my mouth. It was too delicious. Opening my eyes slowly, looking straight into his, I noticed they were darker, much more sinful than before. Something had changed, the tension in the air was palpable. But as quickly as it was there, it was gone when a tall, leggy blonde stood in front of him trying to get his attention. She was your typical college girl, perky tits, long legs and blonde hair with a voice that reminds you of a screeching cat...Ugh!

I walked as though I was on a mission. "Just get this over with and you will be fine," I kept telling myself. It's just a music class, but the thought of letting people in and listening to the lyrics that told so much of my pain and hurt, made my stomach churn and my knees weak.

"Come on Neva, you can do this. Do it for him."

Stepping into the empty classroom, I sighed with relief. Worn, dark blue chairs filled the room progressing higher with every row. Taking the steps, I walked to the back row, taking in the rest of the room. It was like any other classroom, but it held so much more significance to me as I sat down on the most uncomfortable chair imaginable. I checked my phone. I had two texts, one from Low and one from Logan.

**Low: You can do it, princess! Love ya! XO**

Low must have known I was feeling off. It wasn't the class itself I dreaded, I just didn't want anyone else to hear my pain through the lyrics I wrote. The nightmare from this morning only magnetized that feeling tenfold. I text her back a thank you and checked the message from Logan.

**Logan: You know you want me! X**

Ha! Smiling, I looked at the time the text was sent to me. It was when he was being mauled by his groupies, asshat! Tucking my phone away, I realized the once empty room was starting to fill up. I pulled out a pad and a pen for today's class and took a deep breath, but before I could release it, a smooth and sexy voice seemed to stop my body from functioning properly.

"Hey...Can I sit here?"

I looked in the direction of the voice and gasped. I was looking at the guy who, just moments before, turned me into a swooning puddle on the ground. His hands were in his pockets watching me as the muscles in his arms tensed, waiting for my answer.

He was the definition of tall, dark and handsome. But it was his eyes that struck me the most. They were multiple shades of blue. I couldn't make out how many, but they bore straight through me, making me oddly edgy, but at the same time weak at the knees. His dark hair fell over the blue pools as he flashed me a sexy smile. He was six foot of pure perfection, wearing low slung ripped jeans and a tight Goo Goo Dolls shirt. He was lickable, edible and oh-so-sinful.

Just say something Neva, anything...

"Erm, uh..." I stuttered.

Great start Neva, how about trying a simple yes?

"Um..."

Jesus! Nod woman. Just nod!

Nodding in reply, he sat down beside me, so close that I could smell the tempting scent of sin wafting from him. He smelled dangerous. I closed my eyes, letting my body take in the scent; it was like sweet tortuous heaven, a combination of strong coffee and mint. What the hell am I doing? He is going to think you're a crazy, weird stalker. Neva, stop it!

I could barely make out what the professor was saying. Something about getting to know each other or some crap like that, but my focus was purely on this man, sitting so close to me it was making my skin prickle.

My thoughts were suddenly interrupted by the professor, shit. What did he say?

"Sorry, could you repeat that?" I asked as my cheeks took on seven different shades of red.

"Name and what you want to achieve while you are here." The professor replied, clearly annoyed at me for not paying the slightest bit of attention.

"Neva James, I, uh...want to teach people the importance of music...." I said in nearly a whisper. Ugh, that was just uncomfortable. Placing my arms on the desk I lay my head down, trying to bring my cheeks back to a normal color as the professor asked the sexy stranger the same question.

"Angel Walker, I want to meet people who understand my passion for music..." He said in a smooth sexy voice, I think my jaw just hit the floor. Turning my head in my arms, I locked eyes with him. Shit, what do I do now?

Reaching out, he pulled my hand out from underneath my head, making me sit up straight in my chair. As soon as his large hand touched mine, I was lost, his touch caused butterflies to swim around in my stomach.

"Nice to meet you Neva..." He said in a slow sexy whisper. Oh shit, I think my panties just melted.

Come on Neva, you need to say something. Anything!

"I, um..." I started stuttering again, oh God.

Come on Neva!!

"It's nice to meet you too, Angel." I finally said as I shook his hand, which sent shocks of electricity through my veins.

The rest of the class went by far too quickly. There were moments where Angel's arm would brush mine accidentally, causing goose bumps to rise quickly, covering my pale skin. For a reason I couldn't describe, I wanted him to keep doing it, I wanted to bask in the deliciousness that was Angel Walker.

"Assignment is on the board. I want you to write down your feelings, be it happy, sad, excited or depressed. I want you to write them down, think of it as a diary. You have three weeks to complete it." Time stopped. I couldn't think or breathe. This was my worst nightmare, the thought of telling a bunch of strangers how I felt, scared the crap out of me, this is what I was trying to avoid. This was my idea of hell on earth.

"Until next time, Neva," Angel said, interrupting my own torturous thoughts, his smooth and sexy voice wrapping around my name. He placed a kiss on the back of my hand, and I think I whimpered. What the hell? Pulling me out of my own self-pity, my heart fluttered from the softness of his lips against my skin.

"I, uh. See you around, Angel." I said, only slightly stumbling over my words.

I hurriedly made my way to the front of the class, trying to watch my step and not to fall over on my ass as I made a beeline for the door. I had to get away from Angel. I wasn't fooled by his name, and he definitely didn't come from heaven. Everything about him screamed sin, but something about him had gripped me and I wanted to know what it was.

"Oh, yeah you will." Angel replied from the back of the class with a sexy smirk. Shit!

*Three*

I DIDN'T NEED A MIRROR TO tell me my whole body was multiple shades of red. Angel Walker was just something else, he screamed bad boy. Even his name was sexy and wicked, Angel Walker.

Pulling my head from the gutter I checked my phone, one new text.

**Low: The spot X**

The spot was a picnic bench near the football field. Low says she picked it because it had somewhere to sit, but I knew she picked it because she had a perfect view of all the hot and sweaty guys taking their t-shirts off before they hit the showers. I replied to let her know I was on my way, my mind quickly drifting back to Angel. The way a single dimple adorned his sculptured face when he smiled, his husky laugh and his intense eyes. I was hooked.

"Hey darlin.'" I jumped as Logan whispered into my ear,

placing his arm around my shoulders giving me an unexpected shudder, what the hell was that?!

"Shit! You scared the crap out of me, Logan." I pulled his arm from my body as I carried on walking towards the picnic bench, putting some distance between us. Okay, I know he is all kinds of hot but the guy has a man whore reputation. He is a walking STD. I turned to tell him I would meet him at the spot but all I saw was his backside strutting away with another girl clinging to his hip. See? Walking STD!

The meeting spot finally came into view as I passed the football field, the picnic bench was ours, just Low's and mine. Unlike Tate and Logan's meeting spot, there were no 'groupies'. Taking my usual seat on the built-in table, I perched my feet on the seat. Tate had already taken a seat next to me, but today he had his t-shirt off as he soaked in the last of the summer heat. His eyes were closed with both hands stretched to his sides as he leaned back slightly. I decided to take that opportunity to poke him in the ribcage with my finger, pulling a girl-like squeal out of his lips. I couldn't help but laugh as he gave me the dirtiest look for making him sound like a girl.

"Put your shirt back on, dude. I don't want to see that!" I said, still laughing.

But my laughter was quickly stopped as I took in the sight of Logan making his way over to us, shirtless. Logan's chest was glistening with sweat, causing his highly toned abs to stand out brilliantly. He had a body that could make even the straightest of men swoon. I had seen Logan shirtless too many times to count, but today? He looked edible. Even I'm not immune to his devilishly good looks!

What the hell was wrong with me lately? I mean, it's Logan. He is my brother's best friend and my secret protector. Ever since that night we found out about my father, I had nightmares; gut wrenching, take-your-breath-away nightmares, nightmares that would feel so real, as if I was physically there. Sometimes I would feel this sense of dread, suffocating in a subconscious hell. There are times I have woken up screaming, finding my face tear-stained from the haunting shrieks that I hear every time I went back to that place.

A year after my father died, my nightmares became more intense, crippling me with fear while I slept. The demons becoming more real, my surroundings clearer, my fears magnified. I was always on the bridge, the bridge where dreams and promises were shattered, causing unimaginable heartbreak. One night, Logan was sleeping over. That night would change our relationship forever. I was back on that damn bridge again, the smell of car fumes filling my nostrils as I inhaled, panicking as the sudden feeling of being trapped once again consumed me. I screamed at the top of my lungs, my throat burning against the brutal force as I tried to escape. But something grabbed me out from the blanket of darkness, pulling me to safety, it was Logan.

Logan must have mentioned the nightmares to my mom, the pain clearly evident on her face as a doctor uttered the words Delayed Onset PTSD. They said I had survivor guilt. My dad had asked me to go to the store with him that night, and I should have been in that car with him, I was supposed to die with him. Instead, he died alone.

Weekly therapy sessions had helped me manage the feeling of guilt that I harbored, but my guilt would be a permanent scar, it would never truly disappear. The nightmares were in a war of their own, flanking me when I would least expect it, dragging me into the depths of hell once more, forcing me to feel the guilt.

As the years rolled by, the nightmares slowed, gradually making less of an appearance in my life. The only time I have any nightmares now is if something triggers them. One of the last times I had a nightmare was when a horrific car crash had killed a whole family. The news had broadcast the wreckage, showing the carnage that was left behind. I haven't watched the news since.

"Hey guys." Logan said as he took his seat on the bench "Where's Low?"

"I am right here, man whore!" Low shouted as she stomped up behind him, pulling him off his seat by his wrist. She plunged her finger into his chest, "You need to either keep it in your pants or stop screwing my damn friends, Logan!"

"What are you squealing about now, Low?" Logan said with his eyebrows raised, taunting her.

"I just had Erika crying on my shoulder because you didn't call her after you screwed her, twice!" Low spat, I winced. Logan was going to get his ass kicked by Low and it wasn't going to be pretty.

"Which one's Erika again?" Logan asked, clearly amused by Low's sudden outburst as he chuckled, taunting her further.

"Ugh you're so freaking disgusting, Logan!" Low spat, exasperated knowing she was fighting a losing battle. Taking her probing finger out of his chest, she took her place on the picnic bench and sighed. "I'm not finished with you, Logan White." she muttered.

"So, Ace is having a party tomorrow. Who's in?" Logan said

rubbing his hands together with a perfect smile on his face. Ugh, a frat party was the last thing I wanted to think about, especially today of all days.

"Count me in, dude." Tate replied only opening one eye, clearly enjoying the heat against his skin.

"Neva, do you want to go?" Low asked. Turning to my friend, she looked really excited and she was pulling out the puppy dog eyes. Damn, how could I say no to that?

"Sure, listen I have to be somewhere, I will meet you back at the dorm, Low." I said trying to catch Tate's attention as Low nodded in understanding "Tate, are you coming with me?" I asked knowing what his answer would be. I was met with a brick wall of silence. I sighed. I knew he wouldn't want to go, but I had to ask him anyway.

It was ten years to the day that my father was cruelly taken away from us. The pain was still there, just not as raw as it once was. I miss him every day, especially now I am older, but I could never seem to get Tate to come with me, I didn't know why, maybe it was just too hard.

"I am finished for the day so I am going to head out." I said standing up "I'll see you guys later." I said as I started making my way towards my dorm room.

"Hey Neva, wait up!" Logan called from behind me. Turning around, I couldn't help but stare at his overly muscular body twisting and contracting as he ran towards me, sweat adorning his masculine chest.

"What's up?" I asked as we started walking, making our way through the throngs of students.

"Do you want a ride?" He asked, putting his t-shirt back

on before placing his hand on my shoulder. He stopped me mid stride as he looked into my eyes, giving me silent understanding. I had never learned how to drive, it was just something I didn't want to do for obvious reasons. I also hated getting into a car, Logan and Tate were the only people I trusted to give me a ride and I was thankful Logan understood that today, I needed him.

"Sure." I said "Thank you Logan." He understood why today was so important to me. No one should have to live without their father, no matter what their age. Logan understood it more than most, his dad left him and his mom when he was just three years old. Being an only child, Logan only had Tate to lean on for any type of male role model in his life.

I tentatively got in the Jeep that Logan and Tate shared and buckled my seat belt. Logan started the engine as he handed me his iPod to pick a song to play. I swiftly found the one I was looking for. It was the beautiful sound of guitar strumming that hit my ears first, slowly followed by the sweet soulful voice of Dave Mathews Band as he sung the heart-shattering lyrics of "Crash into Me".

Logan's smooth voice flooded my ears as he quietly sang the lyrics of the song that held a deeper meaning to me. It was one of the first songs I ever tried to replicate with my dad's guitar. It took me endless hours trying to get it right as I adjusted my fingertips, trying desperately to find the right notes. I have loved the song ever since. Looking out of the window, I saw the familiar long, winding roads that adorned glorious landscapes of perfectly green blades of grass with the most beautiful wildflowers bursting with vibrant colors. Logan didn't need to ask the directions or where we were going, he knew without even having to confirm it.

Familiar and distinctive trees surrounded us, arching as they reached amazing heights, enclosing us in an amazing vision of summer. Disappearing into a tunnel filled with never-ending shades of green, highlighted by the magnificent rays of sunshine, we made our way down the winding road to the place that held so much significance to my family.

It was the lone standing wooden swing, gently swaying in the warm breeze that I recognized first. I realized I hadn't been here in so long that it made my heart hurt. The grass was trimmed back and the flowers in the flowerbed that was placed underneath the tree, were magnificent. A single fence that surrounded the plot, separated it from the adjoining farm fields that housed horses and cows. Memories of many family days flooded my senses as I took in the place that brought so much happiness and so much sorrow. My dad and I had stumbled upon this place on one of our day adventures in the car and I was mesmerized with it. Dad must have felt the same way, because only a week later he bought the plot of land from the farmer who owned it and put up the separating fence, and even installed a small wooden swing. We would spend hours on that little plot having picnics and playing silly games. Tears filled my eyes as Logan parked the Jeep in a space near the plot.

Taking a shaky breath, I looked over at Logan, whose face was a picture of sadness. I smiled at him, trying to reassure him that I was okay. He nodded in reply, his silent signal letting me know that he was there if I needed him. Stepping out of the Jeep, I made my way over and took a seat on the ground next to the large tree. We had scattered my dad's ashes here, it was a place we all loved and we knew he would feel at home here. Taking a deep breath, I tried to swallow the lump already forming in my throat.

"Hey, daddy." I said in a whisper "It's been ten years since you were taken from us and it still hurts, it hurts so much." Sighing, I pushed the pain away, trying to block it out. "Logan is here too. I'm sorry Tate couldn't come, he is just as stubborn as mom. Mom is doing okay, but you already know that, I can see from the plot that she has already been here." She was always fussing over us. A lone tear escaped my eyes. I swiftly wiped it away before continuing, "I love you so much, daddy. God, I miss you so much." Tears streamed down my face as the lump in my throat tightened, causing sobs to escape my mouth as I broke down with my face in my hands.

I was suddenly aware of warm hands wrapping round my waist as a strong body held me from behind. Logan's head rested on my shoulder as he tried to comfort me, like he had done so many times before.

"Hi Brandon." Logan started "I have to tell you, your daughter is one strong woman. She has had to deal with so much in her life and I know that you would be so proud of her, but she thinks I can't see it, the pain and the sorrow. It's there in her eyes. I am going to take her home now, I'm sorry we didn't stay long, but it's so hard for her. We will see you soon." Logan finished, causing gut-wrenching sobs to escape me. I was suddenly in Logan's arms as he carried me to the Jeep, holding me close to him.

I noticed Logan had turned the music down in the Jeep, but as he placed me in my seat and made his way around to his, I could hear the beautiful voice of Jason Walker singing "Cry". As the lyrics tore through my soul, causing the tears to fall harder,

I tried to hide my face under my hair to stop Logan from seeing me as a quivering mess.

"Hey." He said softly, moving the hair out from my eyes and tucking it behind my ear "Please don't hide from me, Neva," he pleaded. His face twisted in pain. It was as if he was feeling the pain for the ten-year-old me and pain for being unable to fix it. Ever so slowly he took me by my waist, pulling me on his lap. I could still hear the lyrics from Jason Walker, singing as if the song was made for us in this moment. I threw my face into Logan's neck, sobbing uncontrollably as he tried to soothe me, comfort me, and take away my pain. Large hands smoothed my hair away from my face as I drenched his t-shirt in ugly tears. Pulling back, I looked at this man who was so frustrating but so perfect.

Suddenly, he was too close. His deep brown eyes were filled with unshed tears as if feeling my pain, trying to pull the pain away from me. His hands slowly made their way up to my face, taking it into both hands as he wiped away my tears with the pads of his thumbs. I couldn't breathe, I couldn't focus, but if he stopped, I don't think I could take it. He slowly ran his fingers through my hair, pulling me closer, so close I could feel his breath against my lips, sending shivers through every fiber of my being.

"Neva." He whispered, before ever so slowly pressing his lips against my own, sending a slow-rising heat through my body as he slowly ran his tongue along my bottom lip seeking entry, silently pleading with me.

Logan White was kissing me. I was delirious in a lust filled haze that blanketed the pain I felt just moments ago. I finally let him in, exploring my mouth as he slowly stroked my tongue with his, claiming me. Suddenly, he was no longer the boy who protected me in my darkest hours, or the boy who had a reputation with women. This was someone new, and my God I wanted to know him.

He moaned into my mouth as I let the lust engulf me in a way that made me want him just as much as he wanted me in this moment. We were all tongues, lips and hands as the temperature in the Jeep sizzled between us. I had never been kissed like this.

This was so wrong. I was kissing Logan only moments after sobbing into his neck. What am I doing? Pulling back, I broke the kiss. Searching his eyes, I tried to find a hint of just what he was thinking.

"I'm sorry Neva." He said bowing his head. "I don't know what came over me, I'm so sorry." How could I stay upset with that? It was a moment of madness, weakness or just insanity. I didn't know which, but what I did know is that I didn't want it to spoil our relationship as friends.

"It's okay, I was just as much to blame Logan. Let's just put it down to high emotions and a moment of weakness?" I asked, trying not to hurt his feelings even though all I could think about was that kiss. Stop it, Neva!

"Logan, can you take me to my mom's house?" I asked, hoping to take his mind off what had happened. But he just nodded in response, clearly still reeling about what we had just done.

The drive to my mom's was uneventful, but all I could think about was that damn kiss. The way he held my face so softly, the way he kissed me as though he was worshiping me. Touching my lips with my fingertips, I could feel how swollen they were, bruised from such a luscious kiss, pushing my mind into over drive. There was no use denying it, I loved that kiss.

Logan pulled the Jeep into my mom's driveway, which pulled me out of my thoughts as he killed the engine, making the Jeep seem oddly silent. I couldn't move, it felt as though my heart was keeping me in my seat, willing me not to leave. Turning to look at Logan, his head rested against the steering wheel with his eyes closed, causing his dark lashes to rest against his cheek bones.

"Are you okay, Logan?" I asked tentatively, not knowing how he would react.

"What? Yeah sorry, long drive," He said by way of explanation, as he brought his head up from the steering wheel, adding his breathtaking smile for good measure.

"Good." I smiled, knowing that we were okay made me feel much better "So I will see you at the party tomorrow?" I asked.

"Yeah, I'll see you there Neva." He said as he ran his hand through his hair, causing it to stand on end, making him look even more impossibly sexy. Stop it, Neva!

Nodding, I jumped out of the Jeep, waving at Logan as he drove away, making his way to the dorm he shared with Tate. Sighing, I started walking towards my mom's porch, running that kiss over and over in my mind. Shit!

*four*

"NEVA, IS THAT YOU SWEETHEART?" I heard my mom holler from the back yard, she must have heard Logan's truck pull up.

"Yeah, it's me, momma." I shouted, staring up at the two story house that stood before me.

After dad died, our world was turned upside down and inside out, mom was struggling and was such a mess for so long. The heartbreak was like a dark smog resting heavily on her shoulders, the unforgiving turmoil she was facing was apparent, both physically and emotionally.

It was a couple of days after my father's funeral when I noticed something was wrong. Suddenly, Tate was cleaning the house, ironing clothes and cooking dinner. He had taken some of the extra weight from mom to help her cope, to help her grieve for the husband she lost so tragically, and far too soon.

But mom's grief started taking its toll on us, the house, the bills, our relationships. Tate tried to help as much as he could, but he was still just a kid himself. He picked up a paper route and gave mom all the cash from that just to make ends meet. He used his weekends to clean cars and mow lawns just to earn that little bit extra for mom, to try and keep a roof over our heads. But the cracks were showing quickly. Without my father's income and mom not being able to get out of bed some days, the bills started to take over.

Tate was freaking out, I had no idea what was going on, but he was saying something about having to move away and leave all our friends behind. On top of the grief we were trying to get through, this was something we didn't need. I remember a man coming to the house, I didn't know who he was, but he had a business suit on and didn't look too happy. Tate pulled me away from the door and told me to go to my room, stopping me from seeing the man. But, I was intrigued. I sat on the staircase, watching as Tate slammed the door in the man's face. My brother's tears threatened to spill, wiping his nose quickly with the back of his sleeve. A mixture of pain and anger quickly taking over his features, he picked up a pile of papers and charged up the staircase, his footsteps loud against the wooden floor above me. I quickly realized he was in mom's bedroom, the usual loud creak of her door penetrating my ears. I don't know what Tate had done or said to mom that day, but only three hours later, the house was up for sale and mom was back in the kitchen, cooking.

In six weeks the house was sold, the bills were paid, and we had moved into a smaller house just three streets away. To this day, I still have no idea what Tate had said or done when he walked into mom's bedroom, but what I do know is that whatever happened...He brought our mom back.

Now, standing on my mom's porch, I looked over the house that we lived in as a family of three. It was just as stunning as the day we moved in. The white panels showcased large bay windows on the bottom story, while smaller matching windows lined the second. A large, wooden porch wrapped around the entire house, enfolding around it perfectly, as if embracing it in a warm hug. Moving my gaze, my eyes landed on the beautiful front garden. It was pruned and weeded to an inch of its life, but my God, I never tired of seeing the amazing Technicolor of flowers that lay perfectly within the soil. I smiled, knowing my mom would have already pruned and watered the front garden and was now probably in the back doing the same thing.

"Can you bring me the Lavender on your way around, sweetie?" Mom shouted, pulling me out of my thoughts. She must've heard me walking towards her.

"Sure, momma."

Mom had picked up gardening as soon as we moved here ten years ago. She said she needed a hobby, I guess it was her way of keeping busy when she wasn't working. Before dad died, she had worked as a successful project manager of a large interior design firm, but when tragedy struck our family, mom left. Once the house sold and we paid everything off, mom had enough money to start up her own small business within the small town. She was now the most sought after interior designer in Spring Water.

Picking up the lavender from the porch bench, I made my way around to the back yard, the scent of the flowers made me smile. Mom always smelt like lavender. Stopping just short of the gate that surrounded the back yard, I watched as mom crouched down on the ground. Digging in the freshly laid soil with a content smile on her face, I stood and admired the woman who had done so much for Tate and me since my father's death.

Lorena James was stunningly beautiful, with naturally wavy, blonde hair and piercing green eyes, she was striking. Even with the amount of baking she does, she still manages to keep her perfect figure that matches her 5ft 6in frame.

I watched as she stopped digging and took in her garden, smiling. It seemed she had an eye for landscaping too. The garden was by no means huge, maybe around a fifth of an acre, but with mom's design ideas she managed to make it look a lot bigger. She had planted a wide range of flowers, all perfectly arranged by color and tone, which trailed down the left side of the garden, while on the right stood the small oak tree that held a lot of memories. The tree was surrounded by a man-made pond, with its own mini waterfall. It was breathtaking. And when the sun fell, the whole garden would light up with beautiful little fairy lights. It was mom's little piece of paradise.

"Here you go." I said, kneeling down beside her on the ground.

Her blonde hair was pulled back into a messy up-do, the loose strands of hair framing her gorgeous face, but keeping it from hiding her beautiful eyes. She wore faded jeans that were ripped at the knees, with an old college shirt that showed off her perfect curves. She may be digging up mud and getting her hands dirty, but she still looked awesome.

"Thank you darlin." She said before sighing, the southern twang in her voice raspy from the humid air. "No Tate?" She asked, not once taking her eyes from the ground as she carried on making holes for the lavender to be placed in. She knew he wouldn't come, but she still asked every time.

"I'm sorry." I could only apologize for him. I had no idea why Tate stayed away from mom's. He would only come around on the holidays, and even then it was only because I forced him. It was like he didn't want to acknowledge mom. I hated having to watch the disappointment flash before her eyes. I have no idea what goes through that head of his sometimes.

"It's okay." She muttered, clearly upset. "So, how is school?" She asked, swiftly changing the subject.

"Interesting." I replied, watching as she placed a small lavender tree into one of the holes she had dug.

"Oh, how so?" Oh, shit. My answer had clearly caught mom's interest, and she was using her 'discreet' way of finding out what we were up to. I wasn't falling for it.

"Oh nothing much, I met a couple of guys, had hot and dirty sex on the football field with Coach Carter, got drunk on beer and whiskey and bet fifty bucks that I could become pregnant before the week is out...." I trailed off.

"Neva James!" She shrieked, dropping her spade and whipping her head around into my direction. The shocked look on her face was so dramatic that I couldn't hold the laugh that was ready to escape my mouth.

"I'm sorry, but that was just too easy!" I said, gasping for air between laughing so hard at my mom's reaction.

"That wasn't nice, Neva." She scolded, desperately trying to keep a straight face before giving in and laughing along with me, holding her stomach as she chuckled. "You know I worry about you guys." She said as she pulled me in for a hug, the sincerity in her voice disarming.

"I know." I mumbled, understanding her need to protect us. We were all she had left, and when Tate doesn't show up...It hits her hard.

"Come on, I made lemonade." She said, pulling me up from the ground, her hand wrapped within mine as we walked through the patio doors and into the house.

Stepping straight into the kitchen from the back yard, the room quickly cooled my skin from the humid air outside. Toeing my boots off at the door, I smiled as I watched mom put her apron on. A grin on her face as she moved around the kitchen effortlessly, pulling out the scales for measuring out flour for her next creation. She slowly wiped her powder-covered hands on her apron as she set the flour aside, bending down to open the oven door. My nostrils suddenly awakened as I was hit with the most heavenly scent, chocolate. Peering over her shoulder, she revealed hot, mouthwatering chocolate cupcakes. The scent alone took me back to a time when we were a family of four, the day of my seventh birthday. Dad was setting up streamers and balloons in the garden of our old house, quietly cursing to himself as he pinned his thumb for the sixth time that morning. Mom was in the kitchen fixing up all the party food, while Logan and I were hiding out in my room, sharing one of my mom's incredible cupcakes.

Mom had warned each and every one of us that if we touched any of the food before the guests arrived, she would never make chocolate sponge pudding again. It was a threat we all took seriously. But I couldn't resist mom's cupcakes, they were completely out of this world. Deciding to take a chance,

I sneaked into the kitchen when nobody was around, quietly making my way towards those tempting cupcakes, when I heard someone clear their throat. Turning around, I saw Logan, both hands behind his back with a cheeky grin spread across his face. Slowly his hands came into view, showing me exactly what he was hiding. Two chocolate cupcakes, one for me and one for him.

"Honey, did you hear me?" Mom asked, ripping through my thoughts.

"Oh, sorry mom. I zoned out, what did you say?"

"I said a letter came for you, it's on the table." She replied, shaking her head and rolling her eyes at me.

"Oh, thanks." Picking up the letter, I quickly glanced at it before stuffing it into my pocket, I'll open it later. I just wanted to sink my teeth into one of those out-of-this-world cupcakes.

But before I could take a bite, my phone suddenly chimed, alerting me to a new text. Pulling my phone from my pocket, I slid my finger across the screen, revealing a text from Logan.

**Logan: Need a ride home?**

I had to re-read it twice. I thought he was going back to the dorm?

**Me: I thought you went home?**

His reply was immediate.

**Logan: Went for a drive. Ride?**

Smiling, I replied, feeling thankful that there was no weirdness between us.

**Me: Sure.**

**Logan: Be there in 10.**

**Me: Mom made cupcakes.**

**Logan: Be there in 5...**

I grinned as I placed my phone back into my pocket. Logan had the biggest sweet tooth ever, especially when it came to my mom's cupcakes.

With a minute to spare, Logan pulled up just as I was hugging mom. Tears formed in my eyes as she held me tighter, as if she didn't want to let go. I needed to come home more often, I hated mom being on her own.

"I'll call you soon, mom." I said as I pressed a kiss to her cheek.

"Okay sweetie." She said before turning towards Logan. "Drive safe."

We all knew the meaning behind those words. Mom had sold the car after dad died and hasn't stepped foot in a car ever since. Relying solely on buses and trains couldn't be easy, but she made it work, never once complaining.

"Bye, mom," I said over my shoulder as I made my way around to Logan's Jeep and climbed in. Smiling, I waved good-bye to mom, tightness pulling at my chest as I noticed wrinkles sitting at the edges of her eyes, the brightness of the summer sun forcing me to take notice. How had I not noticed them before? The pain and suffering she has to endure daily from the loss of my father had clearly started to take its toll on her. Blowing a kiss out of the window, I sighed as we pulled out of the driveway and headed back to campus.

"Got you a present," I said turning to Logan, revealing a chocolate cupcake that I had been hiding behind my back, just like he had done all those years ago.

"Thank you." He smiled, taking the cupcake out of my hands before sinking his teeth into the chocolate centered cupcake.

I watched as he chewed, this throat muscles moving as he swallowed, making my heartbeat flutter.

Sitting back in my seat I was trying to control my increasing heart rate when I felt something land in my lap. Looking down, a smile slowly formed on my face. It was half a cupcake. Turning my gaze to Logan, I couldn't help but notice a saddened expression on his face, his brows furrowed as he tapped his thumb against the steering wheel.

"You okay?" I asked. He only nodded in response, keeping his eyes trained on the road ahead.

The rest of the drive was silent, the air becoming thick and prickly between us. It was weird. I was just about to ask Logan what was going on when he quickly turned on the radio, blasting some sort of rock music I had never heard before.

The silence was still there when he pulled into campus. He clearly didn't want to talk about it, so I didn't press him.

"See you later, Logan." I said as I got out of the car.

"Yeah," was the only response I got from him before he reversed the truck out of the parking spot and sped off campus. Weird.

Sleep didn't come easy that night, there were no demons to trap me, only Logan's soft lips, trapping me with earth-shattering kisses.

*five*

THE DORM ROOM THAT I SHARED with Low was just your regular box room. Two single beds lined the back wall with only a single bedside cabinet separating them. It was tiny, but it was my home away from home. Low's bed was showered in a mass of clothes, hiding her pink comforter as I could hear her getting ready in the bathroom. I couldn't help but laugh, the place looked like a tsunami had hit. How it was possible for Low not to be able to find anything to wear was beyond me, she had a ton of clothes and always looked amazing in whatever she wore.

"Neva, is that you?" Low shouted as I walked through the door. I placed my bag on my bed, thankful I had finished my last class for the day.

"Yeah, it's me." I replied just as Low walked out of the bathroom looking stunning. Her hair was a mass of curls which cascaded effortlessly down her back. Her makeup was flawless, not too much but just enough. She had to have on the most gorgeous black dress I had ever seen, which cut off mid-thigh, showing off her never-ending legs, finished off with scarlet red heels. They made her seem a lot taller than her 5 foot 4 inches in frame.

"Wow Low, you look gorgeous!" I said in awe as she made her way over to her bed, going through the clothes that still lay in a chaotic mess as if she was looking for something.

"Thanks!" She smiled at me over her shoulder "Aha! Found it." Turning, she dangled a sleek electric blue tube dress in front of me. There was barely anything to it. Seriously, I had bigger belts than that!

"And what exactly do you want me to do with this?" I said raising my brow, inspecting the barely-there dress that she was holding out in front of her chest.

"You are going to wear it tonight for the party." She stated, clearly I had no choice in the matter. I really just wanted to wear some jeans and a concert t-shirt and have a good time, not be the girl who was practically naked at one of Ace's parties. Sensing I wasn't overly keen on the idea, she walked towards me, placing the dress over my right shoulder. "Just trust me, Neva?" She said with a smirk. I knew that look and I knew I wasn't going to get out of this one.

"Okay, but if I don't like it, I am throwing on some jeans and a concert tee." I said, pointing my finger at her. I have never liked drawing attention to myself, it just gave people an opportunity to study me and maybe just one of them might see the real me, the broken Neva that I tried so hard to hide.

Two long and torturous hours later, I was finally allowed to look in the mirror and when I did, I had to do a double take.

Surely the girl in the mirror was someone else? "Christ." I was looking at my reflection in awe while Low stood next to me smiling.

"You look smoking hot, Neva!" Low squealed, pulling me into a hug so tight I could barely breathe. I have to admit, the girl did good. My dark brown hair was free and floating down to my shoulders, a stark change to my usual boring ponytail. My eyes were lined with a perfect blend of midnight black and ocean blue, giving it a dramatic smoky eyed effect. My lips were expertly lined with gloss, and my cheek bones hinted at a subtle rose blush. But it was the dress that Low had done wonders with, it was a perfect match against my pale skin and dark hair. The dress showcased my curves, clinging to my body in all the right places, stopping mid-thigh. I was speechless, I had never dressed like this before, I had never wanted too. My hands suddenly started shaking, appearing at the most inconvenient time. Taking a slow, deep breath, I concentrated on slowing down my rapid heartbeat, telling myself that it was no big deal, it was just a party. Stepping into my black strappy heels, I was ready. Well, physically anyway.

Ace's house was only a five-minute walk from our dorm, the house that had a reputation for crazy parties and drunken students, keeping half of the town awake. As Low and I made our way over, we talked about classes and the teachers. Well, I say talk, but what I actually mean is, listening to Low rattle on about who was the hottest guy on campus. My mind flashed back to the kiss with Logan over and over again, just thinking about it caused butterflies to stir in my stomach, doing absolutely nothing for my nerves.

"There better be some hot guys here." Low said, pulling me

out of my thoughts as Ace's house came into view. The house itself was a two-story red brick building and it was freaking huge! Four tall, white columns graced the front steps that led up to the entrance, which was now littered with people. A mass of cars littered the street with a sea of color, bodies scattered across anywhere they could find space to stand. Tentatively making my way up the steps of the house, my step faltered as nerves hit me once again. Low must have sensed my unease as I felt her hand gently push against my back, walking me straight into the house. We were suddenly in the middle of a makeshift dance floor, filled with bodies grinding against each other as the music from the large sound system made my ears ache in protest.

"Come on, Neva, let's get a drink." Low shouted, the loud boom of the music drowning her out. Placing her hand in mine, she pulled me towards the kitchen, which resembled a bar, as every available surface was lined with various bottles of alcohol. A large table sat proudly in the middle of the room as a group of guys hovered around it, hooting and hollering as they cheered on their friends who were playing an intense game of beer pong. Walking through the kitchen and out of the large patio doors, I saw the guys hovering around a second keg, all holding the same red solo cups. What was it with guys and beer? Making our way over, I darted my eyes around the back yard, noticing that Logan was nowhere in sight. Where was he? My line of sight was suddenly interrupted when Ace Turner stood right in front of me, looking my body up and down. Ugh!

"Well, well, well Neva James...I'll be damned." Ace said with a smirk, He was one of those guys who was the shit, and knew it. Ace was one of my brother's friends. He was sexy if you liked the whole underground-fighter-buzz-cut thing.

"Dude! What the fuck? Leave my sister alone!" Tate said, scrunching up his nose and punching Ace in the arm. Ace only smirked and raised his brow, giving Tate a "you-punch-like-a-bitch" look.

"What? Everyone wants a piece of this!" Ace said, rolling his hips and biting his lip. Could he get anymore pig-headed? Probably.

"Hey, guys." I said, throwing Ace a dirty look. He flashed me his cheeky smile and shrugged his shoulders, taking another mouthful of beer.

Our little group consisted of Tate, Ace, Zane and Colt, all of them just as show-stopping as the next. Tate, Zane and Colt played college football, while Ace was a fighter in the underground. Football season hasn't started yet, but the rumors about scouts coming to watch the guys play were rife, they were *that* good. This, of course, meant they were popular, especially with the woman. Zane and Colt brought a lot of attention due to them being twins, a *very* hot set of twins. Ace was a grade A douchebag, but the women loved him. Rumors about what skills he had out of the cage still haunt me. Yuck. Then of course there was Tate, my brother, named the object of every woman's fantasy three years running. Yeah, college girls really needed to find a hobby, namely ones that didn't involve wondering what my brother was like in the sack. The only person missing was Logan, the star quarterback and panty-melting extraordinaire.

"Where's Logan?" Low asked, looking around the back yard trying to spot him.

"No idea." Tate said, turning to me. "He didn't come back to the dorm last night. He did say he was coming, right?" He asked, as he poured two cups of beer, handing one to me and one to Low.

"Yeah, he said he would meet us here." I replied, shaking my head at the cup that Tate had offered me. Pulling out my phone from my purse, I sent him a quick text.

**Me: Where are you? XO**

Placing my phone back in my purse, I couldn't help but worry over Logan. Was he avoiding the party because of what happened? I smiled as butterflies filled my stomach once again, remembering that mouthwatering kiss. Shit, stop it Neva!

"I saw him at the gym this morning pummeling the shit out of the bags." Zane interjected, taking a gulp of his beer before continuing. "Probably pissed that he didn't get laid last night." Zane chuckled, turning to his twin.

"Dude, she wanted me. What can I say? I'm fucking sexy." Colt declared, the smug tone in his voice making me chuckle.

"You mean we're sexy." Zane scoffed, throwing his twin a dirty look.

"No, I'm sexy." Colt said, pointing his finger to his chest.

"What the fuck? Dude, we're identical twins. If you're sexy, then that means I'm sexy." Zane argued, clearly finding his twin's idiocy amusing.

"I am the older one, therefore I am sexier."

"Jesus, did mom drop you on your fucking head as a baby? What does three damn minutes have to do with how sexy you are?" Zane taunted.

"Dude, you think I'm sexy?" Colt laughed, holding onto his stomach as he bent over. The roar of his laughter drowned out by the booming bass from the speakers.

"Christ, I need a drink." Zane mumbled, slapping his brother on the back of his head before walking into the house.

"Come on Neva, let's dance. These idiots will stand there all night arguing about who is sexier." Low sighed, grabbing my hand and pulling me towards the makeshift dance floor. Looking over my shoulder, I couldn't help but shake my head at the guys.

The pounding bass soon took over my body once we made it to the dance floor, my hips swaying in time with the thundering music, becoming lost in my own little world. Opening my eyes, I looked around for Low, my gaze quickly landing on her brilliant blonde hair. She had her hands clasped around someone's neck, clearly having already found herself a dancing partner. Smiling, I closed my eyes, letting the music take over my body once more, wandering back to a place where I could become lost; not worrying about anything other than concentrating on the movement of my body.

I was suddenly aware of a hand encircling my waist, slowly turning me around. Ready to tell whomever it was to take their hands of me and find another girl to grind up against, but my mind faltered when my gaze locked onto beautiful chocolate brown eyes. The small flecks of green were twinkling under the dim lighting.

"I'm right here." Logan whispered, pulling me towards him. Our bodies aligning perfectly as he slowly directed my hips with his own, his thigh in between my legs, guiding me. I was entranced. His hands moved towards my waist, running those enticing lazy circles in my skin that he had done many times before. But this time, they felt different, more intimate.

I basked in the feel of Logan's hard chest against mine, his hands resting on my body, making my head spin. Questions ran around my mind at lightning speed, trying desperately to find the answers I couldn't seem to conjure. Something had changed. This wasn't two friends sharing a dance at a party. This was 'dance fucking' with a friend...No, he is much more than that, he's...he's, my Logan. I was all types of confused, how had this happened? One minute we were childhood friends and the next we were... what the hell are we? My confusion was suddenly pushed to the back of my mind as the music changed, the speakers now pounding out my favorite song, "Kiss Me Slowly" by Parachute.

I let the lyrics engulf me, the gentleness of Logan's touch swallow me, and his scent control me. Our once grinding bodies now moved with a gentle seductive sway, my head resting on Logan's chest as his arms snaked around me. Holding me close, pulling me into a deeper embrace. Bowing his head, his lips brushed the shell of my ear, pulling a whimper from my throat. His soft, soothing voice penetrated my ears, as he sung the lyrics of the song to me.

My knees were suddenly weak. Everything south of my waist ached as he gently nipped my earlobe. Tightening his grip around my waist, he stopped me from becoming a swooning heap on the floor. This was so confusing, but I couldn't deny that I loved the feel of Logan's arms wrapped around me. I didn't know what this was, but whatever it was...I didn't want it to stop.

We stayed locked in that embrace throughout the rest of the song, swaying together while Logan would intermittently sing certain lines from the song to me. Holding on to his tight white t-shirt for dear life, it was my own little slice of heaven.

As the song drifted into a finish, I pulled back, my eyes locking with Logan's. What the hell had we just done? My mind was filled with so many questions that it took me a moment to notice Logan's reaction, but when I did, I couldn't help but chuckle nervously. He was grinning like the damn Cheshire cat.

"I'm going to get a drink, want one?" He asked, still holding me tight against his body. I nodded my head, completely blown away by his reaction. The smile on his face was disarming, but it was enough to settle the never-ending questions that were running through my mind.

Unwrapping himself from my body, Logan's hands gently cupped my face, placing the most tender of kisses on my cheek. It was enough to make me weak at the knees once more. Reaching out to grab me, he quickly pulled me back into the safe cove of his chest, his scent surrounding me in a safe embrace. Suddenly, my feet were no longer touching the floor, instead wrapped around Logan's waist as he carried me across the room, placing me on a chair to ensure I didn't fall on my ass. He smiled sweetly before making his way out of the room, flashing his trademark smile at me over his shoulder.

I slowly released a breath I didn't realize I was holding, shaking my head as the realization hit me. We weren't alone. Tentatively, I looked around the room, finding all eyes were on me. It was unnerving, my cheeks slowly heated as I tried to avoid eye contact with...well, everyone. It wasn't surprising that people were intrigued by the little scene. Although our relationship had always been platonic, Logan still had a man-whore reputation. My face quickly took on a deeper shade of red as people finally started looking in different directions, carrying on with what they were doing. But one set of eyes didn't leave me. It was as if I could feel them boring into the side of my face, my skin prickling as the hairs on the back of my neck stood on end, feeling a familiar sizzle in the air. Only one person could do that, Angel.

Turning my head towards his scorching gaze, I found myself looking straight into his eyes. It was as if I was staring straight into the bright blue depths of the ocean. But instead of clear, crystal waters, I saw pain, years of pain expertly masked to the prying eyes of others. He was hiding something. I just didn't know what it was. Slowly making his way towards me, he smirked, making him look even more impossibly sexy. I felt as though he was the hunter, and I was his prey, ready to devour me at any given moment.

Suddenly standing before me, my eyes wandered, taking in every inch of him. Low slung, ripped jeans adorned his narrow waist, while a tight, fitted black t-shirt showed off his large frame and lean waist. He looked damn tasty. My gaze finally found its way back up to his face, a sexy smirk pulling at his lips, clearly amused that I was checking him out. But it wasn't his body or his chiseled jaw line, or even his perfectly defined lips that kept my attention. It was those eyes, I could feel them sucking me in, pulling me into places that scared the crap out of me; yet it was turning me on at the same time.

"Boyfriend?" Damn, he was gorgeous. Shit, did he just say something?

"Huh?" How could this man manage to make me forget how to use my brain?

"Is he your boyfriend?" He repeated, his eyes never leaving mine.

"Who? Logan? Erm, no. Why?" I didn't know what the hell Logan was after tonight.

"Good, glad to know there is nothing standing in my way." He said, flashing me a panty-dropping smile. "Dance with me." His voice seemed to take over my body, pulling me into an unbreakable trance. I only just about noticed that I was back on the dance floor with his arms wrapped around my waist tightly, his breath tickling my skin.

We swayed gently, the lyrics of "She Talks To Angels" by The Black Crowes surrounded us. My body quickly covered in goosebumps as Angel played the notes to the song on my back, turning me into his own personal guitar, strumming me expertly. It was so soothing and hypnotic, but at the same time I felt vulnerable. I couldn't put my finger on what it was, but it felt as though this man was pulling my pain and vulnerability to the surface. The thought made me feel nauseous, I didn't need another spectator waiting for me to fall apart. I didn't need another reason to crumble.

The thought pulled me right back to the present, out from under the smoky haze that Angel seemed to have laid upon me. I can't do this. Pushing my hands against his muscular chest, he quickly released his hold on me. I stumbled back, my shoes pinching the balls of my feet. Angel's eyes widened in surprise as he reached out to catch me, his arms swiftly wrapped around my waist, and saving me from hitting the ground.

"Careful baby, no need to fall at my feet." He said, his smooth and husky voice doing delicious things to my panties. He pulled me back up against his body, so close that I could feel his abs tremor underneath his shirt.

"I don't need saving." I muttered, pulling away from him, trying my hardest to stay on my feet.

"Could have fooled me, darlin'." Angel drawled, his gaze never faltering. A lightning bolt of shivers shot down my spine. As he pulled me up right, my eyes darted around the room wondering where Logan could be. He had been gone ages. I smiled sweetly at Angel, thanking him for the dance before quickly leaving the room in search of Logan. I had just stepped out into the back yard when I saw him, sitting on a chair, holding two solo cups of beer with a smile on his face. While Georgia Mathews gave him a lap dance and judging by his face, he was enjoying every *damn* minute of it. A wash of emotions came crashing over me; hurt, pain, jealousy and betrayal, like a knife twisting in my chest. I didn't know what Logan and I were doing, but watching him with Georgia reminded me of exactly what Logan was like. This was him, what he did best. Hot tears stung my eyes as I bolted from the back yard and into the house, desperate to find a place to escape.

Making my way through the sea of people, I found a staircase leading to the second floor. Pulling off my stupidly painful heels, I climbed up the stairs, my heels in one hand while the other barely supported my trembling body. Reaching the top of the staircase, I found a long corridor of rooms lining the second floor. I had no idea what I would find behind those doors, but I didn't care. I just wanted to hide.

I opened the first door I came to, thanking the gods for sparing my eyes when I found it empty. I quickly realized that I had stumbled into Ace's bedroom, which explained why nobody was in here. If they were, Ace would have killed them, and it wouldn't have been pretty. As I walked over to his bed, I took in the room. Three of the four walls were painted a brilliant white while the remaining wall was a deep shade of black. The bed was a queen size, cast iron beauty with black sheets, which expertly matched the black painted wall that it was pushed up against. Turning, I noticed Ace's acoustic guitar propped up against the wall in the corner of the room. As soon as I saw it, I couldn't help but smile. It was just what I needed.

Picking up the guitar, I sat down on the bed, holding it into position. Bowing my head, I ran my fingers down the strings, basking in the feel of them under my fingertips. It had been so long since I last played. I could hear the familiar sounds of the chords as I plucked each individual string, tuning it to the particular pitch I was looking for. Tears stung my eyes as I gently plucked each chord. My ears reacquainted themselves with the slow, beautiful tune of "In The Arms of an Angel." The tune drew me into a place of pain as I lost myself in the haunting melody, quietly humming the song to myself.

I smiled at the sensation under my fingertips, the tingling running through me like electricity. But my smile quickly faded, the room sizzled, and the feeling being watched jolted me; Angel. Turning my gaze towards the door, I gasped when saw him watching me closely, trying to gauge my reaction to him being in the room as I stopped strumming. Leaning against the closed door with his impressive arms crossed in front of his chest, he looked sexy and sinful.

"Don't stop." He said, slowly making his way over to the bed and taking a seat next to me. The command in his voice urged me to pluck the strings, falling back into a quiet hum. I suddenly felt my skin prickle as the raspy edge of his voice graced my ears, singing a beautiful rendition of "In The Arms Of An Angel." I slowly wrapped my lips around the lyrics, allowing the pain I felt to pour from my mouth as we spurred each other on, becoming a painful duet.

Tears were slick against my skin as the last line of the song was released in a shaky breath, as I placed the guitar on the bed beside me before quickly wiping away my tears. I slowly ran my hand down the perfect group of six strings, holding onto the longing feeling that stirred beneath my fingertips.

"You have a beautiful voice, filled with so much pain and sorrow." he said, wiping away a stray tear from my cheek. "I can feel the pain when you sing, Neva, I can feel the heartbreak. Who broke you?" He asked in a soft soothing voice, his gorgeous blue eyes slowly unraveling me.

"My dad died ten years ago." I said darting my eyes to the ground, my vulnerability quickly rising to the surface. Angel seemed to be able to open up old scars just with the sound of his voice. "He tried teaching me how to play," I admitted, my gaze following the neck of Ace's guitar. "I miss him so much." A sob broke free from my mouth before I could even stop it. I placed my hand over my mouth and felt a single tear stroll down the side of my face as I tried to push back the pain of my admission.

"My mom used to sing that song to me." Angel confided, his husky voice providing a great distraction from the tight twisting in my chest. I was intrigued as he stared at the wall in front of us, no longer able to hold my gaze. He quickly sucked in a sharp breath, the obvious painful friction hanging in the air around as he continued.

"My dad was a drunk." He mumbled, the tremble in his voice not going unnoticed as the confession pulled me right out of my own misery. This was what he was hiding, this was what the pain represented in his eyes. But, why was he telling me this? I was practically a total stranger.

"He was disgusting, bad tempered and violent. His anger was mostly aimed at my mom. Shit they used to argue something fierce. After kicking seven shades of shit out of my mom, he would just walk out of the house, leave her there on the floor and go and drink some more." He said, running the palms of his hands over his jean covered thighs. "She would clean herself up before coming into my room, I would be hidden under the covers praying that he would just leave and never come back. She would just kneel beside my bed and just start singing. Her voice was just like yours, Neva, filled with so much pain and suffering from the man who broke her time and time again." He said, prying his eyes from the wall to finally look at me. I was shocked into silence, his story was so heartbreaking, but so comforting at the same time.

"Where is your dad now?" I asked tentatively, unsure whether this was territory I wanted to venture down. I understood more than most about demons, about how they could take over you, taunt you and completely destroy you; never forgiving, never relenting and never giving you a second thought. The demons are your friends, your family, and your enemies. They are everywhere, in your classes, your home, even the coffee shop. But they are the strongest in your nightmares, sucking the life right out of you. Never. Letting. Go.

"Gone." He shot, quickly standing and closing down the

conversation. "You have a unique tone to your voice, Neva. The pain lingers on every word you sing. It's been a long time since I have heard anything like it, have you thought about singing at an open mic night?" He said, swiftly changing the subject. His face showed no emotion besides the hard lines of his lips, knowing I had hit a sore subject. His father was his trigger, like mine, just on completely different parallels.

"I haven't got the confidence to do something like that. I'm not a big fan of having a room full of eyes on me." I muttered, the thought made the pit of my stomach clench violently. Taking a deep breath, I concentrated on Angel, trying to distract myself from the familiar feeling of bile rising from the depths of my stomach. "I wouldn't even know where to start."

"I could help you." He spoke softly. His finger tilting my chin up to meet his gaze. "We could help each other."

"Why would you help me Angel? You don't even know me." I asked. We didn't know a single thing about each other, only that we were both broken in one way or another.

"I may not know what your favorite color is or your favorite movie, but what I do know is the pain in your voice, so beautiful and heartbreaking. I also know the complete peace you feel when you touch the strings of a guitar, because I feel it too." He said, crouching down on the floor in front of me, placing the palms of his hands on my thighs, the innocent touch scorching my skin. "I also happen to know you are very sexy, especially when you blush like you're doing right now." He said, a sexy chuckle escaping his lips, causing my whole body to turn a brilliant shade of red.

Angel's hands started slowly creeping up to the tops of my thighs, the gentle pressure welcome against my skin. Slowly standing, he took a step closer, his eyes locked on mine. I couldn't look anywhere else, they entranced me, pulling me into a place where I didn't know which way was up or down. We were nose to nose, his warm breath tickling my lips. His large, masculine hands cupped my face gently, the rough calluses grazing against my skin as he pulled me closer.

"I also know that right now, I want to kiss you." He said, in a slow sexy drawl. Suddenly his lips crashed against mine, the softness of his lips causing me to gasp. His tongue slowly ran across my bottom lip, searing me with just a single stroke, setting my whole body on fire. Moaning against his mouth, I tasted the bitter shock of whiskey, the sensation turning up my body temperature to boiling. Suddenly his hands were in my hair, tightening as he grasped it into fists, pulling me towards him. The erotic act only helped deepen the kiss, as Angel took control, sending bolts of lightning through my body. But all of a sudden, I was remembering the way Logan's hands caressed my skin softly, the way his lips would gently graze mine, how my body responded to Logan's touch, his slow and deliberate kisses or the way he drew lazy circles in my skin. My head was screaming for Logan, for *his* kiss. But my body was urging me along with Angel, his rough hands against my skin, the way he could control me completely with just one kiss. But now that Logan had penetrated my thoughts, he was all I could think about. I had to stop this, now.

Placing my hands on Angel's chest, I shoved hard, abruptly breaking the kiss. I was panting and breathless, trying to absorb what I had just done. "Fuck." He groaned, placing his forehead against mine. His chest rising and falling as he tried to fill his lungs with air, it seemed as though I wasn't the only one affected.

The distinctive sound of a door slamming shut startled me, someone had seen us. Pushing against Angel's chest again, he slowly took a step back away from my body, his face a picture of confusion. I quickly stood and made my way to the door, gasping as a scent filled my senses making my mouth water. It smelled like spiced apple and cinnamon. It smelled like Christmas. It smelled like Logan.

*six*

I FELT AS THOUGH I COULDN'T BREATHE, questions were swimming in my mind as I pushed back the urge to vomit. What the hell has just happened? I could feel my world slowly tipping on its axis, pulling me in multiple directions. What exactly had Logan just seen? I had to find him and explain, I may not know what was going on with Logan and I, but I needed find him. Turning to a stunned Angel, I smiled tightly. He had moved to sit on the bed, his elbows resting on his knees. Damn he was gorgeous.

"I have to go." I said in a breathless whisper. Angel seemed to sense that something had changed as he walked toward me, his gorgeous blue eyes filled with concern as he stood in front of me. Placing his finger underneath my chin, my whole world began to falter, taking me with it. I stumbled from the sheer intensity pulling between us, my body quickly responding to his touch as he grabbed my shoulders, catching me before I fell into the wall behind me. But this time, his touch didn't cause me to melt. Instead, it felt like a slow tortuous burn. And part of me wanted to stay to see just how far the burn would go, but I needed to run towards Logan. Not only to find out where we stand, but to try and make sense of...well, everything.

"Angel." I whispered, my voice cracking from a sudden feeling of rage that was holding back my voice. My throat felt like a volcano biding its time, building up and balancing on the cusp of erupting. Angel's eyes widened at my response; only moments ago his lips were touching mine. I still felt the searing heat from the kiss on my bruised lips.

"Neva." Angel groaned hoarsely, slowly placing a lingering kiss on the corner of my mouth, a whimper escaping my lips and making me swoon. I had to get out of here, knowing that if I locked eyes with his, I would be pulled in again. I had to find Logan.

"I have to go," I repeated. Angel's eyebrows furrowed in confusion before understanding washed over his features, knowing that I needed to get away. His eyes blazed a dark hue of crashing ocean blue shades, boring into me.

"I'll see you around, Neva," He said, taking a step back. His gaze lingered before opening the door and leaving me in a puddled mess.

I was finally able to catch my breath once I heard the door click shut, the intensity in the room dying down to neutral territory. My legs quickly started to respond to my brain, moving as if ready for a marathon. I needed to get out of here, I needed to find Logan and find out what the hell is going on. My throat was screaming in protest as I could feel the lava build up inside me, pushing my anger to boiling point. Quickly making my way out of the room and down the stairs, I dodged the bodies that were littering the staircase, most of them trying to rip each other's clothes off in a drunken haste.

I needed to find Logan, but I had no idea where he could be, as I got to the bottom of the staircase I was so focused with determination to find him I walked straight into the hard chest of Ace. His hands quickly wrapped around my shoulders to steady me, his eyes took in my body from head-to-toe, checking I wasn't physically harmed.

"Are you okay, Neva?" He asked, clearly concerned by the angry snarl on my face.

"I'm fine, have you seen Logan?" I asked, trying to smile sweetly to reassure him I was fine. He could look scary to any outsider, but underneath the muscles, tattoos and the douche bag persona, he was loyal to his friends, and that meant he was loyal to their sisters too.

"Saw him a couple of minutes ago actually. When you find him, tell him that he owes me for the fucking wall." He said as he pointed over his shoulder. Looking in the direction he was pointing, I gasped. There was a hole in the wall about the size of a fist just beside the front door. What the fuck happened? What had he done? Ugh, tonight couldn't get any more damn confusing. But before I could ask Ace exactly what had gone on, he was already on his way back to the party with two girls under his arms, guys hooting and cheering as he walked back into the kitchen. Rolling my eyes, I made my way out of the front door, the floor cold against my aching feet as I realized I had left my shoes in Ace's room.

As I carefully navigated my way down the steps, I started to look around the people who were in the front yard trying to find Logan. Where was he? I started searching for the Jeep within the maze of cars that were still littering the street. There were fewer cars parked outside than before, but it didn't matter, I could spot that Jeep from a mile away. Walking down the driveway I spotted it, parked further down the road.

As I made my way over, I shuddered from the obvious temperature drop, I wrapped my arms around my waist, hugging my body to try and heat it back up again. I was now close enough to the Jeep to see Logan sitting in the driver's side with his head against the steering wheel, it was now or never. I slowly made my way around to the passenger door, he still hadn't noticed I was there until I threw open the door and climbed in, making him jump and bolt upright.

I was ready to let him have it when I noticed him nursing his hand as it started to swell before my eyes. That didn't look good. Moving quickly, I pulled his hand into mine to inspect the damage, it was just as I had expected, the dumb ass had punched the damn wall! Logan flinched as I ran my fingertips over his wrist, causing him to pull it back into his lap.

"Don't." He said in a defeated tone, he wouldn't even look me in the eye. What the hell? He had no right to be pissed off with me! My blood boiled as anger shot through me like a raging bull.

"What the fuck, Logan?" I spat, his face quickly snapping around to finally look me in the eyes.

"Are you fucking serious right now, Neva? Why the hell are you angry at me? I wasn't the one nearly fucking another guy on the dance floor while dumb ass here was getting you a drink!"

He shouted as a wash of anger took over his face. "Then, I find you sticking your damn tongue down his throat in Ace's God damned bedroom! Tell me, Neva, did you give it up to him?"

The acid lava building in my throat reached violent temperatures as the volcano engulfed my voice, suddenly erupting with so much vehemence that the words physically hurt as they exploded from my mouth.

"That's fucking rich coming from the man whore who can't keep his dick in his pants!" I spat viciously, the realization hit him like a car. "Yeah, I saw your grope and grind session! I hope it was fucking worth it because yet again, you think with your damn cock!" My whole body was shaking with fury as hurt flashed in Logan's eyes, but just seconds later it was quickly taken over by the look of rage.

"What the hell are you talking about, Neva?" He screamed, wincing as his hand jolted from his sudden movements.

"Don't play the dumb card with me, Logan! I know what I saw, I walked out back to find out where the hell you had gone, but it was fucking obvious when Georgia Mathews was practically dry humping you like the dog she is!" I shouted, pointing a finger in his chest. Looking down at my finger, he swiped it away with his good hand, suddenly looking up at me with a smirk on his face. He was fucking smirking!

"No Neva, what you saw was a wasted Georgia looking for a lay! She was so wasted that Ace had to call her damn brother to come and get her." He said, lowering his voice a notch as he rolled his eyes, I didn't care if Georgia was wasted. My anger was still there.

"You loved every minute of it, Logan, I saw your damn face!"

I spat, I was so close to slapping that ridiculously beautiful face of his.

"Yes, I did." He stated flatly causing tears to sting my eyes, the anger quickly simmering as the pain crept in. I couldn't look at him anymore, his eyes were slowly breaking my resolve. I suddenly felt Logan's hands on my face, wincing as the hurt cut deeper, forcing me to look into his eyes as tears fell to my face relentlessly.

"I loved every minute of it because a girl kissed me today in this very Jeep." He said, his words like daggers slicing me open, forcing me to bleed. "And then she came to this party dressed in electric blue, leaving me so breathless, it hurt. Then we danced and I felt like I was flying." Sobs escaped my mouth as Logan pushed away the tears that just kept coming. "I loved every minute of it because all I could see was you, all I could feel was you. But then I saw you watching me and I hadn't even noticed what Georgia was trying to do until I threw her off my lap to find you and explain." He paused before taking his hand away from my face, instantly missing the physical contact. Sighing, he continued.

"But then I found you kissing another guy, and all I felt was rage; and I stupidly took my anger out on a wall. I was insanely jealous, Neva." He took in a shaky breath as he ran his fingers over his injured hand.

Panic engulfed me at Logan's words, I hurt him. That realization felt like the daggers from before were now twisting painfully in my chest.

"I'm so sorry." I croaked through sobs, reaching out to touch Logan's face. But when my palm met his cheek, I sobbed harder.

He leaned into my touch, closing his eyes for just a moment, only to snap them open and pull away from me.

"I need to go and get my hand looked at." Logan said, looking down at his injured hand, wincing as his skin changed from a perfect bronze to a vast range of blues, purples and blacks within minutes.

"I'll go with you." I said, reaching around for my seat belt. This was my fault and I had to fix this.

"No, Neva." He said, stopping me from buckling in. "I'm going to do this on my own."

"What? Why?" I asked, confused. I didn't understand.

"I just need some time to work some things out in my head." He said, shrugging his shoulders.

"Okay, when will I see you again?" I said, the vulnerability evident in my voice.

"Soon, I promise. I just need some time." He said as he placed his forehead against mine. "I will always keep you safe from your demons, Neva, whether they are in your nightmares or too close for you to see."

I understood the double meaning of what he had just said to me. There was no doubt that he thought Angel was no good for me, that he was another one of my demons, sucking me in and forcing me to hurt, just like the ones in my nightmares.

I nodded, letting him know I understood before I made my way out of the Jeep.

"Stay safe, Neva." Logan whispered as I stood next to the Jeep with my hand on the open door, using it to support myself as my body suddenly turned into a dead weight. Flashing him a reassuring smile, I sighed.

"Always," I said. I shut the door and stepped back as I watched Logan drive away, not knowing if or when I would see him again.

*seven*

I WOKE UP TO THE BIGGEST DAMN headache of my life, ugh. The room spun as I pried my eyes open one at a time, taking in my surroundings. My electric blue dress was in a crumpled mess on the floor, my desk chair knocked over. What the hell happened last night? I tried to force my fuzzy head to think back, pushing through the pain in my thundering head. Memories of music, dancing and kissing flashed before me, but they were quickly squashed by the hurtful reminder of Logan driving away, leaving me all alone. He left because of what I did. Tears stung my eyes as I stared up at the ceiling, trying to remember what happened after he left and how the hell I got home.

Suddenly, the most irritating noise known to man was making my head throb even harder. But even though my head felt like it was going to explode, I smiled. The irritating noise was coming from the floor beside my bed. Sitting up and leaning over slightly, much to the protest of my head, I found a passed out

Tate snoring like a damn wart hog with a head cold. Peering over Tate, I looked over at Low's bed to find it empty, weird.

I was completely clueless as to what happened after Logan left, but judging by my sudden amnesia and aching head it looked like it involved a stupid amount of alcohol. I'm never drinking again. But I couldn't dwell on it too much as my head rattled violently. Shit, I'm *really* not drinking again! Standing up, my legs suddenly felt like jelly and my head felt like a train wreck. Wobbling slightly, I took my first step. Really not a good idea, searing pain shot through my temples faster than my mind could register it, oh shit! Taking a staggered breath, I pushed past the pain as I stepped over a sleeping Tate, my bladder begging for relief.

Finally making it to the bathroom, I flipped the light switch on, jumping back in surprise before quietly chuckling to myself. In the tub was a fully clothed Low. She was completely passed out, her chin resting against her chest while a leg dangled over the edge of the tub. But the sight of her clutching a half full Tequila bottle against her chest made me full out laugh, my splintering head pounding harder as Low stirred from her alcohol-induced coma.

Walking over to the tub, I placed my hand around the neck of the Tequila, pulling as I tried to get the bottle out of her grasp, but it wouldn't budge. Low had a vice-like grip around it and she wasn't letting go. I chuckled, shaking her shoulder to try and wake her.

"Pour me another drink." She murmured, clearly still drunk from last night. Rolling my eyes, I decided to try different tactic. Turning towards the sink I picked up a glass and filled it with ice cold water. What? You seriously think I'm going to pass up this opportunity? Snickering, I held the glass up above her head, tilting it slightly.

"Sis." Tate scolded from behind me, shit! Busted. "Do I have to remind you about the time Logan woke you up like that?"

My world seemed to just stop at the mere mention of his name, my eyes crossing and my stomach churning. Suddenly my head pounded harder, my legs throbbed viciously and my chest ached uncontrollably as I felt acid bile rise to my throat, burning everything in its path. The glass fell out of my grasp, shattering loudly against the floor as I scrambled to the toilet, throwing up absolutely everything.

Rule number one: Under no circumstances is tequila your friend.

Tate held my hair back as I threw up everything, including my damn dignity.

Low, of course, slept through the entire thing.

When my stomach finally stopped contracting, I rested my head against my arm, groaning from the amazing feeling of the cool, tiled floor against my flushed skin, using the toilet to prop me up.

I must have nodded off because when my eyes opened again, I saw Tate cleaning up the shattered glass from the floor. Looking over at Low, I noticed she was no longer clutching the bottle of Tequila, Tate must have managed to pry it from her vice grip. She was still out cold, snoring softly as the leaking tap dripped slowly onto her bare leg. This girl is going to feel like absolute death if we don't move her from the tub.

"Tate." I croaked, my voice protesting from the after burn of my make out session with the toilet bowl.

"Don't worry, I've got it." He said as he looked over his shoulder at Low. Chuckling, he swiftly picked me up into his arms making his way through the obstacle course that was our dorm, gently placing me on my bed.

"You owe me one for this, baby girl." He said, rolling his eyes before making his way back to the bathroom to collect Low. Hopefully he would have more luck pulling her out of her tequila coma than I did.

I wondered what time it was, reaching for my phone from the bedside cabinet I noticed I had two texts.

**Low: You will hate me in the morning! Tequila Babbbbyyy! X**

I chuckled as I realized she had sent it to me last night by way of apology. Shaking my head, I checked the second message. I didn't recognize the number, opening the text I gasped.

**Coffee? I think you will need it after that tequila. Angel x**

Oh shit! Please don't tell me Angel saw me wasted, what the hell happened last night? Closing the text I checked the time, 10:30 am on a Tuesday morning, luckily I didn't have class until 3:00 pm, so I had enough time to try and shake off my hideous hangover.

I suddenly heard life from the bathroom as Low murmured something incoherent while Tate chuckled. I couldn't help but smile at my comatose friend who was nestled in Tate's arms as he made his way over to Low's bed. Ugh, I needed caffeine and greasy food to soak up the tequila.

I opened my text messages back up, desperately holding back the urge to text Logan to see if he was okay. No, he wanted time, so I will give it to him.

**Me: Coffee sounds good, Meet me at the Black Bean Coffee Shop in an hour? Neva x**

His reply was instant.

**Angel: I'll be waiting, A x**

His reply sent a shiver down my spine, stupid shivers!

Low was passed out on her bed with her arm slung over her eyes as she snored gently. God, I loved this girl! Tate was sitting on her bed watching her like a guard dog. I smiled; he had always been protective of us both.

"Tate, can you fill in the blanks? My head is a little fuzzy." Understatement of the year there, Neva! Tate chuckled at me as I slowly rubbed my temples.

"Oh you know, the usual. You and party girl over here got wasted on tequila even after I told you to slow down. You two danced, the guys and I had to fight off the creeps to stop them from groping you. Oh, and Low started dancing on a table while you were passed out cold on Ace's lap!" He said in mock irritation. I just sat there open mouthed. "Then..." Ugh, as if it could get any worse. "Ace and I had to carry your drunk ass's home!" I winced, ugh lovely!

"I'm sorry." I said holding back a giggle. "Can I make it up to you with caffeine?" I asked, he smirked raising his right eyebrow at me. "Okay, coffee and a blueberry muffin?" He flashed a smile at me as I chuckled. The best way to my brother's heart was definitely through his stomach.

Pulling myself off the bed, I made my way to the shower, stopping inches away from the door. Looking over my shoulder, I watched my brother lace his fingers through my best friends.

What the hell?

"I'm meeting a friend at the coffee shop so I might be a while. You okay watching Low?" I asked, making him jump as he pulled his hand from Low's. Interesting.

"Sure, just don't forget my muffin." He muttered, his cheeks turning a brilliant shade of pink. Hmm.

"Okay, I'm going to grab a shower and head out." I said, picking up some clothes from the closet and making my way into the bathroom.

The water felt amazing against my skin as I stood directly underneath the heat, my mind running into overtime as Logan's words replayed in my head over and over, again.

*All I could see was you, all I could feel was you.*

The truth in Logan's voice was disarming, but it didn't change anything. He was who he was and I needed to remember that.

Stepping out of the shower, I quickly towel dried my hair, pulling it out of my face with a hair tie. I never cared much for dressing up and wearing a lot of makeup, it was only Low who could transform my face like that. So today I opted for a discreet look, a light coating of mascara, a dusting of pink blush and a single coat of gloss. Throwing on a pair of faded skinny jeans that were so tight they felt like a second skin, and a vintage Guns and Roses concert tee, finishing it off with my white converse.

When I was finally ready, I checked the bathroom mirror to see the damage of the, not-so-smart, tequila hangover.

*What are you doing, Neva?! It's just coffee, right?*

Rolling my eyes at myself I made my way out of the bathroom, checking on Low and Tate before I left. I suddenly stopped mid-stride, Low's head rested on Tate's chest while his hand was on her waist in a tangled embrace. They had clearly done it many times before.

Coffee first, questions later.

*eight*

THE COFFEE SHOP WAS A SMALL little cafe only a fifteen minute walk from campus. It boasted black, iron vintage tables with matching chairs scattered out on the sidewalk, while white wash walls hung classic black and white portraits. A beautiful black silhouette flower mounted on canvas was the center piece on the feature wall, while remarkable black and white images of Marilyn Monroe scattered the remaining walls, it was gorgeous. The building itself was stunning, painted in a pastel mint green and teamed with black lace stencils, showcasing the large bay windows. It stood out perfectly.

Rounding the corner, I spotted Angel sitting outside with one of the large bay windows behind him, the light reflecting off it and giving him a striking white halo that wrapped around his body, framing him beautifully. But it wasn't the angelic halo surrounding him that stopped me mid-stride, it was his eyes. They seemed more intense as the reflective glow illuminated them, bringing them to life.

A slow, sexy smile appeared on his sculptured face as he spotted me. I couldn't help but smile back. He really did look like an angel. He stood up as I made my way to towards him. He wore ripped jeans that were all kinds of sexy, with a black, buttoned down shirt. His sleeves were rolled up to his elbows, showing off some seriously hot, muscular forearms. But then my eyes landed on his boots, there were black and well-worn and the bottoms of his jeans were tucked into them. If they weren't sexy, I didn't know what was.

As I got to the table, he raised his perfect right brow at me before leaning in and whispering into my ear, "How's the head?" I nearly melted in to a puddle right there on the damn sidewalk!

"Fuzzy." It was the biggest word my delicate brain could come up with as I took a step back.

"I didn't order yet, I didn't know how you take your coffee." He said, his eyes never leaving mine.

"Usually I drink a latte, but after last night I need it black and strong." I said. Oh, welcome back brain! A smile tickled his lips as if he found my reply amusing.

"Yeah, I'll bet." He said with a sexy smirk. "Sit, I'll fetch us some caffeine." I nodded, my brain rattling from the sudden movement. As Angel made his way inside to get our drinks, my eyes landed on his backside, giving me the perfect view of his ass. Oh my!

Taking a seat at the table, I rested my arms in front of me, folding them on the cold table as I placed my head on them, trying to stop the painful throb in my head. My mind suddenly flashed back to Logan and the word of warning he had given me about Angel.

*I will always keep you safe from your demons, Neva, whether they are in your nightmares or too close for you to see.*

Okay, so Angel was intense and yeah, his eyes were hauntingly hypnotic, but he was nothing like the demons in my nightmares. I wasn't blind, he wasn't an angel either, which made me want him more.

"Coffee?" Angel's voice pulled me out of my thoughts as I looked up to find him smiling at me, holding two large cups of coffee. Damn, he looked edible.

"What are you smiling at?" I groaned as the smell of coffee filled my nostrils, making my mouth water. Angel placed the coffees on the table and took the seat next to me, this thigh lightly brushing against mine, sending sparks through my body.

"After the amount of tequila you drank, I'm not surprised you feel like shit." He said, shaking his head with a soft chuckle.

"Yeah, about that," I said as I could feel the blush slowly creep across my face. "Can you fill me in? I don't remember seeing you after you left."

"Damn, you were wasted," He said with a mischievous smile. "I came back to check and see if you were okay, but when I found you, you were on the dance floor in your own drunken little world, shaking that sexy ass of yours while your friend was having the time of her life dancing on a table!" I rolled my eyes as he threw his head back and laughed, a deep, throaty laugh. Damn. "Then you couldn't stand up straight and ended up passed out on some guys lap while some other guy threw your friend over his shoulder and took you both home." He said with a shrug as I sighed with embarrassment.

"Ugh, my friend who was dancing on the table – that's Low, we have known each other since forever and we share a dorm room. The guy you saw throwing Low over his shoulder – that's my older brother, Tate. And the guy whose lap I was unceremoniously passed out on – that's Ace, my brother's friend and it was his house party." I said as I brought the cup of coffee to my lips, basking in the heat as the scorching, heavenly liquid made its way down my throat, slowly clearing my head.

"Well, I had no idea who the guys were, so I followed you back to your dorm. Then I realized Tate was your brother when you shouted at him for trying to take your keys because you couldn't open the door. Only a sister would call a guy 'penis breath.'" He said as he laughed hard, causing my mouth to hang wide open in horror, making a mental note of that name for future purposes. *What? It's funny!*

"But I didn't see you, did I?" I asked wincing, why did I drink the damn tequila? Never, ever again.

"You didn't see me because you didn't need to. I just wanted to make sure you got home safe." He said, his voice taking a serious tone. He made me smile, my guardian angel.

"Okay, can we talk about something else other than my drunken misadventures?" I asked, feeling embarrassed.

"Sure, how about we talk about why you ran after I kissed you?" He asked, his eyes glowing.

"Well shit." I said, completely surprised by his forwardness and quick subject change. He laughed at my response, damn I love that laugh. "Do we have to talk about that?" I pleaded.

"Fuck yes, we do, I'm kinda feeling emasculated right now and we need to talk about it because I want to kiss you again."

He said with such confidence that I was instantly turned on, shit.

"Honestly I have no idea why I ran."

*Yes you do Neva, just say his name.*

"I'm sorry I bruised your ego, do you need me to rub it better?" I said with a smile.

*Neva James you are playing with fire!*

"Baby, you can't say shit like that to me." He said on a groan. "Do you have any fucking idea how tempting your damn lips are?"

"I don't know, maybe you should show me." I said as my eyes drifted to his lips which looked so damn edible right now.

He smiled before wrapping his fingers around my neck, pulling me closer, stopping just mere inches away as he slowly ran his tongue over my bottom lip, and sealing his lips over mine, causing me to quiver from his touch as he growled. "So damn sweet."

As soon as his lips touched mine, thoughts of Logan's lips on mine flashed before me, the way his kiss could be as light as feathers but still give me chills, or the way he would whisper my name. But Angel's kiss, this kiss was completely different. It was filled with a mixture of vulnerability and dominance. It was so erotic, sinful, raw and carnal.

I was playing with fire and I could already feel the burn. It was scalding, and I loved it.

The erotic sensation of Angel biting down hard on my bottom lip pulled me out of my Logan-filled thoughts as I moaned into his mouth, spurring him on as I opened my mouth, giving his eager tongue entry to explore. He tasted amazing. The mixture of coffee and pure sin was so damn erotic. The taste of coffee was bitter against my tongue. Angel was just like coffee, strong, bitter, and so damn delicious. His kisses were like a caffeine high, racy, unhinged and oh, so addictive.

His tongue struck mine playfully, causing me to groan as I took his tongue between my lips, taking control. As I sucked on his tongue, Angel made the sexiest noise I had ever heard, a deep throaty moan. I couldn't hold back anymore. I laced my fingers around his neck, brushing my fingertips through his hair, he moaned in response, causing me to smile against his mouth. Feeling confident, I raked my nails through his hair as I scratched his scalp, taunting him, pushing him. It must have worked. I felt his palm quickly find the base of my back, pulling me closer.

His fingers splayed out on to the curve of my back before slowly traveling upwards, brushing my shoulder as both hands rested on my face. It was enough to snap me back. The reminder of Logan touching my face exactly like Angel was doing, danced before my eyes. Quickly pulling away, I broke the kiss as Angel groaned in protest.

"I'm sorry." I apologized, looking straight into his amazing eyes. "I've got to go. I need to get ready for class." I said, trying to hold back a smile as I noticed Angels lips were now lined with my gloss. Reaching out I ran the pad of my thumb over his plump bottom lip, causing Angel's eyes to light up and sparkle as he took my thumb between my teeth and bit the pad, hard. I drew a breath before he soothed the sting with his tongue.

"I'll see you tomorrow in class." He said, taking my thumb out of his mouth with a 'pop' before making his way down the sidewalk.

*Breathe, Neva!*

Staring at my now lukewarm coffee, I decided against drinking the rest of it. I will never be able to drink coffee again without thinking about tasting it on Angel's tongue. I checked the time on my phone, 11:15 am, good I still had time to get Low out of her coma and start the inquisition.

Walking into the coffee shop, I made my way to the counter, ordered two strong coffees for Tate and Low and, of course, a blueberry muffin. Suddenly, there was an ear piercing shriek that rattled through my brain, bringing back the banging throb of my hangover. Turning around, I spotted Georgia Mathews cackling with a group of over-enthusiastic girls, all wearing matching designer clothes. Gag me!

Georgia Mathews was your typical rich bitch, her dad had a lot of money – practically owned half of the town, her mother was a 'socialite' – Whatever that meant! And Georgia gets whatever the hell she wants, that included endless trips to the salon, spa weekends and really expensive shopping sprees. She would look half decent if she just toned down...everything? Today her salon aided blonde hair, fell loosely down her back, her face was flawless with minimal makeup, she was around 5ft 7 in heels, and she had a figure of a model and the fashion sense of one too. Oh, and let's not forget the money to go with it.

I couldn't stand her. Georgia and Logan had dated when they were in high school, but Logan broke it off when he walked in on her with another guy while she was on her knees. How classy!

*Was that a hint of jealousy I could feel? No, of course not.*

"Logan." Georgia shrieked, as I snapped my head round to see a very worn out Logan with his hand in a bandage.

*Oh shit, what do I do now?*

He wanted 'time' and we were standing in the same damn coffee shop. Only now Logan was here with her.

"Hey, baby." The words stung as I registered Logan's voice. I looked over, big mistake, and felt tears sting my eyes as Logan planted a kiss on Georgia's lips. I needed to get out of there. My world was spinning, but I couldn't tell if it was the after effects of the tequila or from what I just saw. There was no time to question it, I needed to leave.

I quickly paid for the coffees and muffin and made my way to the door with my head bowed and my eyes fixed to the floor, avoiding any eye contact. When the door finally came into view, I sighed with relief that nobody had spotted me. It was only when I got outside that I looked over my shoulder. I nearly split in two watching Georgia kiss Logan's face, I needed to go. I couldn't look at Logan a moment longer. I walked away from the coffee shop without a backward glance, knowing that if I did, I would crumble.

*nine*

I WAS IN A DAZE AS I MADE MY way back to the dorm room, only when I reached SWC I slowly cracked, as sob escaped me as I took the stairs to the second floor, needing the enclosed space of my room. When I finally got in there I found a still-passed-out Tate sprawled across Low's bed as I heard the shower running. Ah, the tequila zombie has awoken. Thank God, because I really needed my best friend right now.

I quickly wiped away a stray tear that had escaped. I didn't want Tate to see me crying, the last time he did, he kicked the crap out of some boy because he pulled my hair. I dread to think what would happen if he found out that Logan and I had kissed.

Tate was still snoring like a damn fog horn as I made my way over to my bed. Placing the coffees on the bedside cabinet, I quietly got onto Low's bed, crawling into the nook of his arm and placed my head on his chest. Reaching out for his hand I placed my hand in his, interlocking our fingers together. I used to love doing this with dad. He was always so warm and comforting, and right now, I needed to feel close to him, and Tate was the next best thing.

When dad died, Tate tried his best to take over the role of man of the house. He would cook, clean and make sure mom wasn't a quivering wreck while getting me ready for school. He did an amazing job of looking after mom and I. I loved him so much for it.

Tate stirred and groaned in his sleep, I chuckled and gave him a quick peck on the cheek, which made his eyes open quickly and look to my direction.

"What's wrong, baby girl?" He asked in a sleepy voice as him arm tightened around me.

"Nothing, I'm fine...I just needed a cuddle." I said, trying to hide the crack in my voice. But Tate must have heard it as he sat us up on the bed quickly, looking me straight in the eyes.

"Something is wrong, you've been crying." He said as he wiped away the moisture from underneath my eyes. "Who do I have to kill?"

"Nobody, I'm fine."

Lie.

"Just cramps."

Another lie.

But my answer seemed to make him smile as he moved to open Low's bedside cabinet and pull out some pain killers, throwing them to me before giving me a kiss on my forehead. God, I love him!

Placing my head on his shoulder, I closed my eyes for a moment, only to flick them back open again when I heard Tate groan. I quickly realized what he was groaning at when I noticed him watching Low walk out of the bathroom in nothing but a skimpy towel.

"Why is everything so damn loud?" She asked. Taking my head from Tate's shoulder, I couldn't help but notice my brother eye-fucking my best friend.

Rubbing her temples, Low slowly made her way to the closet for some clothes. No amount of coffee was going to clear her hangover. But mine felt like it was slapping me right back in the face when Tate said the one name that could stop my heart instantly.

"Anyone hear from Logan? He's not answering my calls and Ace is blowing up my phone about the hole in his wall." He said, looking concerned. Logan and Tate were more like brothers than best friends.

"Nope, why did the ass punch the wall anyway?" Low asked from the closet.

"No idea. Have you spoken to him, Neva?" Tate asked turning to face me, oh shit.

"Erm, yeah. I saw him at the coffee shop this morning." I said as I watched my brother stuff his face with the blueberry muffin, completely oblivious to the battle that was going on in my head. "He was with Georgia." I added.

Tate instantly started choking on his muffin while Low came out of the closet, looking at me wide-eyed.

"What do you mean 'he was with Georgia'?" Tate asked when he had finally stopped choking.

"Exactly what I said, he was at the coffee shop with Georgia."

"He wouldn't go there again, would he?" Low asked as she

scrunched her nose in disgust.

"No, he's not *that* stupid." Tate deadpanned. "Are you sure they were there together?"

"Look they are either dating or just screwing. Logan kissed her and called her 'baby.'"

As soon as his name left my lips, my voice broke. No I can't cry, not in front of Tate. But Low must have suspected something when her head snapped to my direction, oh shit. This isn't good.

"Tate, I need to get some things ready for class, can you call me later?" Low asked, turning to my brother. Well, if I didn't know Low and Tate were together before, I certainly do now!

"Sure, laters." He called as he pulled me from the bed, giving me a quick hug. He walked out of the door, leaving just Low and me. I quickly stopped breathing when Low's serious eyes met mine, crap!

Grabbing me by the wrist she sat next to me on the bed. I couldn't look at her, but I could feel her eyes on me, willing me to talk.

"Spill, Nev." Low said quickly, grabbing my face in her right hand, forcing me to look at her. Sighing, I didn't know where to start, but I knew Low wouldn't give up until I told her what was going on.

"I kissed Logan." I blurted out, pulling my face out of her hands and standing. I was sure I heard her whisper something along the lines of 'holy shit'. Oh yeah, holy shit was right, but there was more and I needed to get it out, I needed to tell somebody.

"And I kissed Angel." I said as I started pacing, looking over at Low, who was obviously having a hard time taking in what I had just revealed.

"Tell me what you're thinking, Low. Please?" I pleaded, I needed her to understand. I really needed my best friend right now.

"You need to give me a minute to process this. I'm still kind of shocked you kissed Logan, never mind Angel." She said, still wide eyed at my revelation.

"Why are you surprised about Logan and not Angel?" I asked. I certainly didn't visualize the conversation going like this.

"Logan is a grade 'A' man whore and a complete ass, he has shown how much he is those things after running back to Georgia after kissing you!" She said, her voice rising a few octaves. "But Angel? Christ, he's just sex on a stick. Plus, he has that whole bad boy thing about him, yummy!" She added while fanning herself.

But she didn't know what I did to Logan to make him run back into Georgia's arms, she didn't understand what happened. I don't think I understand it either.

"You can't blame Logan for that, it was my fault." I said, watching her closely as she raised her eyebrow in question. "He sort of saw me kissing Angel." I said as I buried my head in my hands.

"Hey, this isn't your fault, Neva. Look at me." She said, while prying my fingers away from my face. "Did Logan ask you out?" She asked, no he didn't. I shook my head. "Well then, he is an even bigger ass because he is just jealous that you kissed Angel and no doubt that scene in the coffee shop was to make you jealous." She said pointing her finger at me.

"What do I do now?" I asked, God this was stupid.

"That's up to you, Neva. But just remember a leopard never changes its spots."

She was right, why would Logan change for me? There was no doubt I wanted Logan, to feel his lips against mine again, but I will not be made the fool. But I wasn't finished with Low just yet.

"Thanks Low." I said giving her a hug before pulling back to look at her in the face with a stern expression. "So how long have you been screwing my brother?" I asked as I watched a blush cover her from head to toe. Wow, I had never seen Low blush in all the time I had known her.

"Oh God, I'm sorry. Are you mad at me?" She asked, looking like she was about to cry.

"Of course I'm not, I think it's sweet." I said reassuring her. After all, if anyone could put my brother in check, it was Low. "I just wish you would have told me sooner."

"I know, I'm sorry. I just didn't know how you were going to react, plus we haven't been together long."

"Okay, just don't hurt him, Low." I said, even though Tate was a pain in the ass, he was still my brother.

"I won't, I promise." She said with a smile. "So anyway what are you going to do about Logan and Angel?"

"Ugh, I have no idea." I said as I pulled out my phone, I needed to head out to class. "I've got class, but when I know what the hell I'm going to do, you'll be the first to know." I said, giving Low a quick hug before heading out of the door.

"Think with your head not your heart, Neva." Low called after me as I shut the door, right now I didn't trust either of them.

*ten*

**Angel: Dinner at 7, be ready at 6:30. I'm coming for you, Angel x**

CHILLS WASHED OVER MY BODY as I re-read Angel's text for the ninth time in the last hour, it was so unexpected and I loved that about Angel. Everything with him was in the moment, intense and scorching hot. I read the message again, reading the command followed by a seductive threat. It pissed me off, but turned me on at the same time.

Damn, everything about this man turned me on.

From his deep, husky voice, his gorgeous blue eyes and every time I was near him he tied me up in knots. But when I was with Angel, all I could think about was Logan and that kiss. But then it would be all crushed when I am given the painful reminder of how I hurt him and how he is hurting me.

It had been three long and torturous days since I saw Logan

at the coffee shop with Georgia, I hadn't seen him around campus or with Tate either. It shouldn't bother me, but it did. My head hurt from all the unanswered questions swimming in my mind.

My class had finished an hour ago but I didn't want to go back to the dorm. I needed time to think so I came to 'The Spot'. Campus was quiet, only a few cars littered the parking lot near the football field. It was 5:00 pm, which I only knew because I couldn't help glancing from Angel's text to the time on my phone, the minutes slowly ticking by.

I was suddenly pulled out of my thoughts by a familiar cackle. Looking over to the parking lot, I quickly found the source of the ear-bleeding laughter. Sitting on the hood of Logan's truck was the vulture, Georgia. I wish I hadn't looked, but now I had. I couldn't look anywhere else.

Georgia's long, toned legs were wrapped around Logan's waist, his head in the crook of her neck, playfully biting her. My hand wrapped around my already restricted throat as I imagined Logan biting down on my neck, before kissing the hurt and trailing his tongue from the base of my throat, licking lazily right up to my ear.

Shivers engulfed my body as I imagined Logan's lips on mine, soft but demanding, moist but able to leave my throat so dry, as if I was stranded in the desert desperate for just a tiny taste of water.

I was panting, breathless and flushed from head to toe. I watched as Logan so intimately took bites out of Georgia's neck like a man starved. I shouldn't be watching, this was so wrong. But why couldn't I look away?

Sparks exploded through my body as I watched the

nakedness of Logan's back muscles come into view, his shirt all but ripped off as Georgia raked her perfectly polished nails down his beautifully sculptured back. Goosebumps covered every inch of my body as I watched each individual muscle contract under her nails, every muscle in my body clenched as I heard a carnal moan escape his lips. I just couldn't look away, this was so wrong. I should be repulsed, I should want to go and rip that skank from Logan and kick the crap out of her, I should stop. NOW!

The sudden sound of Jason Walker singing "Shouldn't be Good in Goodbye" sliced through my thoughts like a knife, my phone was ringing in my hand loudly. Shit. My hands fumbled as I tried to get the damn thing to shut up, falling out of my hands and tumbling to the ground. I frantically dived for it, the ground scraping my knees as I reached for my phone so I could silence it. But before I could reach it, a strong, masculine hand wrapped around my phone and picked it up off the ground.

I was on the floor on my hands and knees, staring at the ground beneath me. I didn't want to look up. If I did, I wouldn't be able to control the overwhelming urge to tackle him to the ground. I just didn't know if I would kiss him senseless or kick seven shades of shit out of him.

"Neva." Oh God, even the way he said my name was so damn hot. Finally prying my eyes from the ground, I looked up to find Logan crouched down beside me. Dammit, he looks sexy. His t-shirt was now back on and his hair had that hot, messy look to it. But it was his sexy smirk that caught me off guard. *Really* caught me off guard.

"What do you want, Logan?" I asked in a whisper, snatching my phone from his hands.

"You were watching me?" He asked with fire in his eyes. I could feel the heat rising from my toes as my whole body blushed in response. The question was so innocent, yet it was laced with a command so erotic that it practically dripped sex.

"Your silence speaks volumes." He said, flashing that sexy smirk at me once more before quickly leaning in, stopping just before his lips could touch mine. His breathing was erratic, matching mine as my pulse quickened as the seconds slowly ticked by. We sat in this position, both not leaning in for a kiss nor breaking apart. The tension was killing me, I wanted his lips on mine so much it hurt, why wouldn't he kiss me? Tears stung my eyes as I slowly realized he wasn't going to kiss me. He was slowly torturing me. I was so desperate for his touch that a single tear slowly fell from my face. Logan's eyes went wide in surprise, couldn't he see he was killing me? Couldn't he see that I just wanted him to hold me?

I felt the pad of Logan's thumb gently brush the stray tear away, making my blood boil and my panties wet. He was finally touching me, but only to wipe away the tears he had caused, that I had caused, that we had caused together. This thumb lingered on my cheek as he rubbed those delectable lazy circles in my skin, distracting me. I closed my eyes, basking in the feel of such a small amount of skin against mine. His thumb quickly pulled away, only to be replaced with a kiss so soft it was barely there. My eyes snapped open, he was almost screwing that skank on the hood of his Jeep only minutes ago, how dare he touch me like that!

"I saw you at the coffee shop, with Georgia." I spat, my brain-to-mouth filter decided to switch itself off. It just came out so quickly.

"Like I saw you at the coffee shop, with Angel." He shouted "You were kissing him again!"

"Yeah, and you were practically fucking Georgia on the hood of your damn car!"

"And you threw yourself at some guy only minutes after I fucking kissed you!" He said harshly.

"Screw you." I spat, scrambling up to my feet, knocking Logan on his ass before taking off towards my dorm. I could hear him shouting my name behind me, I couldn't do this.

Taking out my phone I quickly wrote out a text.

**Me: I'll be ready, Neva x**

Low was right, a leopard never changes its spots.

I had an hour before Angel was coming to get me for dinner but I was still angry and so shamefully turned on, everything south of my waist was throbbing with need. Logan was seriously fucking with my head, bending me, torturing me, breaking me at a painfully slow pace and all I could do was hold on for the ride.

I walked into an empty dorm room, Low was nowhere to be found and the only sign of life was her messy bed. Sighing, I threw myself on to my bed, face first, burying my head into my pillow. Anger erupted through me, how fucking dare he?! I didn't know whether to laugh or cry at Logan's antics, but my body decided to choose for me. Loud, ugly sobs burst from my mouth as I remembered Logan's touch against my cheek, the way he said my name and the way his lips felt against my skin.

I had to calm down, my thoughts had been so consumed over Logan for the past couple of days that it was making me dizzy. Then there was Angel who was so intense, so sexy and so domineering that I couldn't help but submit to his commands, his kisses, his eyes.

Sitting up on the bed, I mentally kicked myself for letting Logan treat me like one of his whores, picking me up only to let me crash right back down. I needed to stop thinking about Logan and move on. He wasn't mine and was certainly never going to be either, no matter how much I wanted him to be.

Taking a deep breath, I wiped away the tears before getting up from my bed. Making my way over to the closet, I tried to find something to wear. Angel hadn't said anything about where we were going, I was excited but nervous. Would I be able to shut off my Logan-filled feelings for just one night? I could only hope. I was sick of him constantly taking over my thoughts.

It was time to take some control.

After a ridiculous amount of dress changes, I finally decided on a simple LBD with a sweetheart neckline, resting perfectly just above the knee. It was one of Low's. Normally I would dress in jeans and a concert tee, but tonight I wanted to look good for Angel. Pairing it with some sexy, fire-engine red heels and a small amount of makeup, I left my hair free to spill against my shoulders.

I was just re-applying a coat of gloss to my lips when I heard a knock at the door, butterflies soared in my stomach from the knowledge of there being one very hot specimen of a man on the other side of it. Angel was uniquely beautiful, with a chiseled jaw giving him a rough, sexy edge. Coupled with his piercing eyes, he was the bad boy of every woman's wet dreams.

Opening the door, my eyes suddenly traveled the length of Angel's hot body, my jaw instantly hitting the damn floor. The

Adonis that was Angel Walker stood in front of me, dressed in black slacks and a dark blue button down shirt. Leaning his arm against the door frame, he looked damn edible. I couldn't take my eyes off him. Angel was no doubt stunningly handsome, but right now it was his eyes that were making me squirm, they were boundless. Standing in the dull light, they looked like Tanzanite, a passionate mixture of deep blue and striking violet – they really were a rare gem.

"Hi, beautiful." He said in a slow, sexy whisper.

Damn this man could knock me off my feet with just a simple 'hi'.

I swiftly snapped shut my gaping mouth as I willed my brain to help me out, come on brain I know you are in there!

"I, um. Hi." Smooth brain, real smooth!

I could already picture the 'do not disturb' sign being hung in my mind, normal brain function was clearly not happening tonight.

Angel chuckled softly, clearly amused by my stumbling, making me blush a perfect crimson.

When it came to this man, I was a stumbling mess.

I suddenly sucked in a breath as Angel's hand landed on my waist, pulling me flush against his hard, strong body. I reached out, placing my hands on his unbelievably toned pecks, oh God. Angel's other hand quickly wrapped around the base of my neck as he lowered his lips to my ear, making me pant with anticipation.

"You look so fucking beautiful right now. I have to have a taste." He growled before taking my ear lobe between his teeth, pulling out a moan from deep inside me. His tongue gently tasted my skin as he made a trail of kisses from my ear, over my jaw and finally landing on the corner of my mouth. Cool air replaced his mouth as he started to pull away, my body humming and telling me I wanted more. So much more.

My arms flew around his neck as I pulled him back against my body, a salacious gleam appearing in his eyes as I trailed my tongue across his bottom lip.

"So damn sinful." I whispered before locking my lips with his, causing him to chuckle against my mouth.

His chuckling soon ceased when our tongues collided and danced together, entwining in an erotic embrace. Logan's face danced before my eyes, but I wasn't going to let him consume my thoughts. Not tonight, not ever. I quickly pushed him to the back of my mind, hiding him away in a box labeled never to be opened.

Tonight I just needed to feel wanted and needed, not be treated like a piece of glass.

"Wow." I mumbled as I pulled back from his lips, they were just so tempting. I could quite easily sit here for eternity kissing this man, but I knew if I didn't stop this kiss we wouldn't ever leave for dinner.

"You ready?" Angel asked with a satisfied smirk on his face, making me blush. Again.

"Just give me a minute, I'll meet you outside." I said.

I needed a bit of breathing space, this man could leave me breathless with just a damn kiss.

I walked into the bathroom and looked into the mirror. Gloss had smeared around my mouth from the intense kiss Angel had planted on my lips. The arousing throb from my lips was making other places throb simultaneously, mostly places below my waist.

Taking the wash cloth from the sink, I started wiping away the remaining gloss, there wasn't much point putting on some more if our kisses were going to be that intense. I couldn't wait.

Taking a deep breath, I made my way out of the dorm and down the stairs to the main entrance. Looking around for Angel, I wondered what tonight would mean for me, for Angel...For Logan.

*eleven*

Standing on the sidewalk outside the dorm, I quickly sucked in a breath.

I couldn't believe my eyes. Angel was sitting on the hood of the sexiest damn car I had ever laid my eyes on.

Light reflected from its sleek, black, polished body. It was the type of car that could get most men hard just from staring at it. From the glistening chrome to the unmistakable mustang badge, it was an awesome machine. But holy hell it looked like molten sex with Angel sitting on the hood.

My eyes slowly trailed down his beautifully defined body. His muscles bulging against his tight, black slacks as his legs crossed at the ankles. His arms crossed in front of his chest, making his shirt tighten against his magnificently broad chest and shoulders.

Damn I would buy the damn thing if he came with it!

"See something you like?" Angel asked in a smooth, sexy

drawl, clearly indicating at the double meaning in the question.

"Yes, I do." I said with a salacious grin.

I slowly made my way over to Angel who was now showing off that sexy smirk of his that said 'I know you want me'. This man was all kinds of hot and sexy and my God did he know it! Standing toe to toe with the Adonis himself, I placed my hand on his muscular right arm, trailing my nails down his forearm before placing my hand on the hood of the car. "I just don't think it would fit in my bed." I said innocently, my eyes roaming his body before looking down at the car.

"Tease." Angel chuckled, moving off the hood and making his way to the passenger side of the car and opening the door, indicating for me to get in.

I instantly froze. All the blood in my body quickly drained and ran straight to my ears, throbbing dangerously. The familiar feeling of being trapped quickly consumed me, my hands shaking and my body trembling.

I couldn't get in that car with Angel. I was so wrapped up in teasing him that actually having to get into the car was an afterthought.

After my dad's accident, I couldn't even step foot in a car. The thought would fill me with so much fear and dread that I would completely freeze. It wasn't the actual driving part that would send me into a trembling wreck, it was just a small part of it. It was the foreboding fear of the unknown that got to me, what if we got hit? What if there was someone drunk driving right now? It took me years just to sit in a damn stationary car, never mind letting someone drive it while I was in it. When it came to being in a car with someone there was only two people I could trust, Tate and Logan. It was Logan who took me out for my first drive, we only went around the block but it was a huge achievement for me. I was so proud of myself, but I won't get in a car with anybody else.

"I, um, I...can't." I stuttered, completely overtaken with the feeling of fear and dread that I couldn't get my voice to work. Angel grabbed me, clearly alarmed at the look of sheer panic plastered on my face as he pulled me into a tight embrace.

Moments passed as my erratic heartbeat slowed to a steady rhythm, still wrapped in Angels arms as his chin rested against the top of my head. We were completely silent, the only audible noise was our breathing. I felt so safe in that moment but also slightly unnerved that Angel could pull me back so quickly, pulling back I looked up into his gorgeous blue eyes that were laced with so much worry, I gasped.

"I'm sorry." There were no other words that I could say to him to make him understand.

Taking my face in his hands he placed his lips over mine, he made no move to take it further. It was as if he was trying to tell me something through the kiss, trying to heal me, trying to understand.

"You have nothing to be sorry for." He whispered against my lips, sending vibrations through my body with just the hum of his voice. Pulling out of our embrace, he placed his arm over my shoulders as we walked away from the car, where are we going? I didn't ask as I noticed Angel deep in thought.

With his arm around my shoulder, we walked in a comfortable silence, making our way into town. Angel still hadn't mentioned the incident with the car, I didn't know whether it bothered me that he hadn't, so I pushed it to the back of my mind as I became more curious as to where he was taking me. I don't think my feet could stand the pinching from my shoes much longer.

"Where are we going?" I asked, breaking the silence.

"The beach." He suddenly took me by the shoulders, spinning me around to face the most beautiful scene I had ever laid eyes on. Spring Water was a coastal town and I had seen the beach hundreds of times before, but never like this. The sun was setting beautifully in a ray of colors from fiery red, shimmering pinks to smooth orange and majestic yellows. The water was as clear as crystal, reflecting intense, radiant colors across the rippling waves that gently lapped against the shore.

As I stood there taking in the gorgeous scene before me, I suddenly felt a hand wrap around my ankle, I shrieked in surprise as I looked down to find Angel on one knee looking up at me, flashing that panty-melting smile. His hand was wrapped around my ankle as he lifted it from the ground, using his shoulder to steady myself. He gently coaxed my knee to bend as he slipped off my platform heel from my now painful feet, placing my bare foot on his bent knee. I groaned in delight as I felt strong fingers knead into the ball of my foot, working out the kinks and soothing the aches. He paid the same attention to my other foot as I basked in the gentleness of his fingers against my skin.

Picking up my shoes in one hand, he held out his other, silently asking me to place my hand in his. But before our skin could touch, he swiftly threw me over his shoulder as I yelped in surprise while he ran towards the sand.

"Angel! Put me down." I screamed, trying to pull my dress down of my increasingly exposed ass.

"No problem." He said chuckling, what was he...

Oh shit!

The taste of salt water hit me first, burning the back of my throat as the water lapped over my head – The ass threw me in! My foot found the sandy bed as I pushed myself up above the water. Standing, I wiped the water from my eyes as I coughed and spluttered.

"Angel, you ass!" I shouted in no particular direction as I still couldn't see from all the damn water in my eyes. I heard him chuckling at my outburst before another wave of water engulfed me as I was still trying to get my vision to clear.

Two large hands wrapped around my waist making me squeal in surprise, finally clearing my watery vision I gasped as my eyes landed on Angel's very naked chest. I saw sculptured muscles, smooth tanned skin and broad shoulders. Hot damn! He even had muscles in his neck! A twinkling caught my eye as I was checking out his neck, it was some sort of silver chain with angel wings attached on a pendent. It was so fitting and it made him look even more damn sexy.

The water was only waist deep, giving me a perfect view of his well- defined 'V' and that mouth-watering trail of hair that traveled from just below his navel to down to his waistband where it disappeared under his black slacks.

Suddenly, my chest was flush against his, instinctively I threw my hands out to steady myself when I found they had landed on some seriously hard and sexy pecks. Reluctantly, I managed to pry my eyes from ogling Angel's hot body long enough to watch his lips slowly make their way towards my ear as I rested my head against his chest.

Angel's husky voice took over my senses, taking me places I had never been before as he sung "Our Song" by Ron Pope, gently swaying us to the lyrics as the water lapped around us.

A moan escaped me as Angel nibbled on my neck after finishing the song, he was just too sexy. Angel's hands slowly made their way up my body leaving a trail of fire against my shivering skin. Taking my face in his hands, he pulled me close, so close.

"Be mine." It was a question and a demand, an erotic demand and all I could do was submit to it as I nodded my head in response, pulling a growl from him before our lips collided, heating my body with desire against the cold temperature of the water. I was delirious with lust as our tongues danced slowly with each other mimicking the slow and sultry dance we had just done only moments before.

Everything about this man was so intense, so engaging, so consuming. I was becoming lost under his spell, feeling myself wanting him more in every way. I wanted to throw away my inhibitions and give myself to him, just surrender to his mercy. I moaned as his tongue flicked against the roof of my mouth causing my body to turn into a torturous mixture of temperatures. My skin was shockingly cold from the freezing water but my core blazed wild heat from just from Angel's lips.

"Cold?" Angel asked with a smirk, my body shivering once again. I could only nod in response, my teeth chattering from the cool temperature of the water.

Angel suddenly picked me up, my arms latching around his

neck as I lay my head against his hot, wet chest. Emerging from the water, he didn't once falter as he walked us onto the sand, picking up his discarded shirt and my shoes, all still with me in his arms. Walking off the beach and onto the sidewalk he slowly placed me back down on my feet, the cold temperature of the ground not helping with the arctic shudders that were running right through my body.

I was shivering from head to toe as my dress stuck to me like a second skin. Angel must have noticed I was uncomfortable as he placed his warm dry shirt around my shoulders, trying to help warm me, but I knew the only thing that would warm me right now was to take the damn dress off.

Giving me a swift kiss on my already swollen lips, Angel placed his palm against the bottom of my back, right in the sensitive curve, giving me chills on top of the ones that were already spreading across my body. Swiftly leaning in, he growled in my ear.

"Mine."

Oh. Dear. Lord.

For a fleeting second, my body erupted in heat, the type of heat that could only be created by him.

We made it back to the dorm quicker than I expected. I was thankful, as my fingers and toes were completely numb from the cold sea water. I pulled Angel's shirt tight against my frozen body, trying hard to warm myself up.

"You okay?" Angel asked as he stopped walking, pulling me in for a hug just outside my building. I nodded as my teeth clattered and my body shook, I had never been so cold in all my life. Placing his hands on my arms, he rubbed them quickly, trying to bring my body temperature back to normal.

Looking over his shoulder, I noticed his car still sat in the same spot where we had left it. Angel must have noticed because suddenly he was kissing me, it wasn't gentle but it wasn't rough, it was a questioning kiss like he was begging me to answer it with my mouth. Our tongues met and glided against each other as he pulled me against his body, still wet from our dip in the sea. I moaned when I suddenly felt his hardness straining against his slacks, which now rested against my thigh. I needed to stop this before it went too far.

Pulling back, I noticed Angel panting as he rested his forehead against mine.

"You don't have to tell me anything you're not ready for me to hear."

He was talking about the car. I owed him an explanation as to why I went all crazy on him for just opening the damn door. Taking a shaky breath I tried to explain.

"I'm sorry, I just have this fear of being in a car. It scares the shit out of me." I managed, noticing Angel watching me closely. "The only time I can be in a car is if Tate or Logan are driving."

It wasn't a lie. I was just omitting the whole truth. I wasn't ready for him to know the rest. I don't think I ever will be.

"Thank you." He said, pulling me into a hug. "You should get inside, you're freezing. I'll see you tomorrow, baby."

Giving me a quick kiss on my lips before I headed off inside.

*twelve*

MY NOW PARTIALLY WET DRESS clung to my thighs as I stepped back into my room, I needed to get out of these wet clothes. Low had already texted me to let me know she was staying with Tate tonight, so I was on my own. I pulled off Angel's shirt that was now wet and crumpled, dropping it on the floor beside me. I reached my arm around to the zipper on my dress. I pulled my zipper down about half way when I heard someone clear their throat, scaring the living shit out of me.

"Need a hand?" I turned to my bed to find Logan sitting against the wall, one knee against his chest while the other stretched out in front of him. His head tilted in my direction with that stupid, sexy smirk. What I would give to slap that smirk right off of his face.

"What the hell are you doing here, Logan? You scared the shit out of me!" I shouted, still trying to get my heartbeat back to a steady rhythm. Keeping my eyes directed at the floor, I quickly zipped up my dress.

"We need to talk about what happened today." Ugh, I didn't need this right now. I just wanted to get in a hot shower and get in bed to relax.

"There is nothing to talk about, Logan." I spat.

I was getting irritated by our constant roller coaster of a relationship, or lack thereof. But as much as he was irritating me, I couldn't deny how sexy he was looking right now. Tight fitting jeans clung to every defined muscle from the waist down, his chest covered in his trademark white t-shirt and his hair had that bed head look, hot and sexy as if he had been running his fingers through it.

Looking up, I noticed he was staring at me as if I just walked out of a mental asylum naked. I rolled my eyes, I needed to get out of this damn dress. Ignoring the look on Logan's face, I opened the closet and pulled out an oversized shirt and some boy shorts, walking quickly into the bathroom. Turning on the shower I let out a breath, I wondered if I just ignored him then he might just go away.

"I think we do." Logan said from the doorway, making me jump in surprise causing me to drop my clothes on the floor. I didn't turn around to respond to him, I couldn't. I knew that if I did, I would crumble.

"Logan, please leave me alone. I'm tired and you're giving me a damn headache!"

Why can't he just leave? Doesn't he understand what he is doing? To me, to him, to us?

I gasped as I suddenly felt Logan's hand on my shoulder, warmth like I had never felt spread through my veins, making me forget about my wet dress and freezing skin.

"I'm with Angel now." I said panting from his closeness.

"He's no good for you, Neva." He whispered against my ear.

I grasped on to the wash basin in front of me, holding on for dear life. I didn't know if it was a reaction to his voice, his touch or that he had just insulted Angel that pissed me off most.

"Don't." I warned

I had no freaking clue what I was protesting against. Don't insult me, don't touch me, don't break my heart? My knuckles were turning white as I tightened my grip, feeling his body mold against mine, his front to my back as he rested his other hand on my waist, gripping me tight.

"You're wet." Logan husked into my ear.

Oh. Dear. God.

The double meaning in his words wasn't lost on me, I would have laughed if I wasn't so damn turned on. Shivers engulfed my body, which of course, Logan noticed.

"And cold."

My legs were beginning to buckle as he ran his nose up and down the sensitive spot behind my ear, pulling me tighter against him. Instantly turning up the temperature of my body to a boiling point as his hardness rested against the crook of my ass.

"Logan." I gasped, my body responding shamelessly from just one touch against my skin. "What are we doing?" I said breathlessly, the heat from the forgotten shower warming me.

My body suddenly bucked in response to Logan's soft lips as they grazed against my throat, slowly raining sweet kisses across my now warming skin.

"I don't know." He said against my neck, the hum of his voice against my throat sent me into overdrive.

He gently nipped my collarbone making my skin prickle, my throat tight and my legs weak. I was putty in his hands. "But I can't seem to stay away."

Oh. Shit.

"We can't do this Logan." I choked.

I was about to turn around and tell him to leave, but before I could, I was suddenly spun around in his arms. We were chest to chest, nose to nose, toe to toe as he ran his hands down to my ribcage, gripping on tightly as if he couldn't let go. Looking into his eyes, I gasped. They were full of fire, heat and need as he gently lifted me from the floor. I wrapped my legs around his waist, feeling weightless as he started walking towards the shower. No surely he wouldn't?

He did.

Beautiful hot water soaked my skin as Logan held me close to his chest, the water cascading over us causing a cocoon of heat, encasing us in our own little piece of heaven. I was suddenly hyper aware of his hardness which now pressed against my soaking panties as my dress rode up higher to my waist, a stream of water rippled between us, giving me a wash of new sensations as my entire body throbbed under Logan's touch.

This felt so right, yet it was so damn wrong. I wanted this man so much it physically hurt, the world could be ending around us but nothing else would matter as long as I was in this man's arms. I wanted his lips against mine, I wanted him to put his hands in my hair and hold on tight, but he still hadn't kissed me.

Why hadn't he kissed me?

"Logan please, kiss me." I said in a panted plea, I was desperate for him and I couldn't control it, nor did I want too.

My words must have done something to him as I suddenly felt the cold, tiled wall against my back as he pressed his whole body against mine.

"I can't." I felt pain penetrate my chest and tears sting my eyes. "I can't kiss you here." He softly placed his fingertips on my lips, making me quake from head to toe from just the gentlest of touch. "If I do, I won't be able to stop." He ran his finger across my bottom lip, slowly placing a kiss on the corner of my mouth making me moan.

"Why are you doing this to me?" I asked in a breathless pant, trying so hard not to let the hot, wet tears I was holding back fall from my eyes. "It isn't fair." My voice broke on the last word. I'm such a horrible person, how could I want a man who was hurting me at every turn when I had Angel, my boyfriend Angel.

The word boyfriend swimming around in my head caused the tears to fall.

What was I doing? What was he doing? This needed to stop, I can't take this anymore. Placing my hands against Logan's chest I pushed hard as I unwrapped my legs from his waist. Looking up at Logan, I registered the startled look on his face, what did he want from me? Anger filled my veins causing my body to shake.

"What? You expect me to fuck you in the shower? I'm not your damn whore, Logan! You have Georgia for that!" I spat, I was confused, I was hurt, and I was a damn fool.

Water dripped from every part of Logan's body, his hair had flattened and was now framing his face which now wore an angry scowl.

"Don't try that shit with me, Neva. Only seconds ago you were begging me to kiss you!" He was right. I was begging him to kiss me. What sort of person does that?

I sighed, this wasn't doing either of us any good.

"I'm sorry, but this…" I said, pointing between us. "Whatever this is, needs to stop. I'm with Angel and you're with Georgia." I said on a shaky breath as I watched Logan take a step closer.

"Is this what you really want?" He asked. "Is Angel who you really want?" His eyes full of fire at the mere mention of Angel's name.

"Yes."

No. Yes.

"I need to hear it, tell me you don't want me, Nev." His fingers lightly brushed against my cheek, I had to hold back the urge to pull him back to me. "Tell me you don't want me and I'll leave you alone." His words hit me like a train. I did want him, I wanted him so much it hurts, but I can't. I'm with Angel and I can't hurt him. I couldn't do that to him. I took a deep breath and looked up at Logan.

"I don't want you." I whispered, cringing at my own words.

I didn't believe the words that had just come out of my mouth, and judging by Logan's face, neither did he. I had to say it for me, for Angel, for us. Logan took a step back, pulling his fingers from my skin as if he had just been burned.

"I'm sorry, but I don't believe you." He picked up a towel and wrapped it around his body before stepping out of the shower, his clothes were completely soaked through, dripping water everywhere. "Stay safe, Neva." He said over his shoulder as he made his way out of my bathroom, out of my dorm, out of my life?

"Always." I whispered knowing that he couldn't hear me.

Angry, ugly sobs suddenly escaped me as I sat on the cold floor of the shower. Pulling my knees up against my chest, I let the water beat hard on my back, trying to take in the enormity of what had just happened.

What the hell had just happened? I mean, one minute I'm agreeing to be Angel's girlfriend and then the next I'm in the shower with Logan. Oh God, this is a mess! Angel is what every girl dreams of, from his slow, sexy drawl to his piercing eyes. But then there is Logan, the cocky jock with his dirty mouth and ridiculously tempting body. Yet he is the only person who truly knows me and the demons I have inside.

My sobs started to slow and my breath evening to a steady rhythm as I got out of the shower, all but ripping the black dress from my now pruned skin. What the hell I am going to do about Logan?

I finally managed to get feeling back in my body after the heat from the shower scalded my skin raw. Throwing on the oversized shirt and boy shorts, I made my way over to the closet. I didn't need any light to find what I was looking for. Feeling around blindly, my fingers suddenly brushed the familiar object as I pulled it from the dark depths of its hiding place, I sighed as relief washed over me.

Walking over to the bedside cabinet that sat between the two single beds, I opened the drawer to find my black leather notebook and a pencil. As soon as my fingertips grazed the sleek leather I pulled it to my chest as I took a seat on the floor, leaning against the side of my bed as I placed the familiar objects in front of me. I took a moment to take in the unique scent of the leather bound book, before flipping it to its latest blank page as I placed the pencil behind my ear.

Tentatively I ran my fingertips along the neck of the guitar, my dad's guitar. It had seen better days, with scuff marks and scratches lining the body but it was just normal wear and tear of something once loved, once cherished. I pulled the guitar onto my lap after crossing my legs, giving it a perfect resting place.

The notes came easily as I strummed my fingertips across the strings, ignoring the bite they caused from not using my pick. No, I wanted to feel, to feel the pain of the memories of my father. I wanted to feel close to him. I would move heaven and earth for just a moment, a cuddle, a question, a *'it's going to be okay'.*

Before I knew it, I was strumming to the song "Thinking of You" by Love and Theft as my mind drifted to Logan once more, the lyrics falling from my mouth in a hoarse whisper, reminding me of what could never be.

I was so lost in that torturous song that I didn't see Low come in until she sat down on her bed facing me, looking like a deer in headlights. Oh shit, my hands stilled as I looked at her waiting, the silence nearly too much to bare.

"Christ you haven't played in a long time, Neva." Low said, playing with her fingers in her lap, she only did that when something was bothering her.

I shrugged, I didn't want to tell her about what had happened tonight but she was right, I hadn't played my dad's guitar in over twelve months. Playing Ace's old acoustic didn't count, I played his to forget. I play dad's to remember.

"What's eating you, Low?" I asked, moving the subject away

from me. Something is on her mind, and judging by her face, she didn't want to tell me.

"Your brother and I got into an argument, no big deal." She said shrugging her shoulders before getting up from her bed and walking into the bathroom. "I'm going to take a shower." She shouted from behind the bathroom door as the sound of the shower drowned her out.

Shaking my head, I started slowly plucking the strings of my dad's guitar once more. I glanced at my notepad, knowing I had to write down something for my music assignment, the thought made me feel sick. Do I really want people to know how I feel, who I am?

Taking in a shaky breath, I pulled the pencil from behind my ear, hovering over the page as I rubbed the pad of my thumb against the thin piece of wood that I cradled in my fingertips. I took a moment to think long and hard about what I should say, what I should reveal.

Closing my eyes, I let my hand take over, writing only five letters.

EMPTY.

*Thirteen*

ANGEL AND I HAD BEEN OUT together a few times since the night at the beach. We had been texting back and forth ever since and he called me every night before he would go to sleep to see how my day had been. It gave me a chance to get to know the elusive Angel Walker.

I learned pretty much from Ace's party that Angel didn't like to talk much about his family, all I knew was that his dad wasn't around and that he lived with his mom, whom he doted on. Every time he mentioned her, his eyes would light up, making them look even more beautiful than they already were. I was starting to learn so much more about him, yet so little at the same time. He was so guarded and closed off any time we mentioned his father. I shrugged it off though, I wasn't exactly forthcoming about my father either.

He had turned up at my dorm with a single rose without any warning a couple of days ago, leaning against my door frame looking sexy as hell while I stood there with my mouth open in an old oversized t-shirt and boy shorts. My hair was piled on top of my head with a pencil holding it in place, my face was bare without a scrap of make-up – I looked like a tramp.

"What are you doing here, Angel?" I asked, trying to hide my face in my hands so he didn't have to see the monstrosity that was me.

"I thought we could go out for dinner." He said, placing the rose on my bed before taking a step towards me. He pulled my hands away from my face and placed a tender kiss on the end of my nose.

"I'm not dressed to go out for dinner." I said, blushing with embarrassment.

"You could go out in nothing but that beautiful shade of red on your cheeks and you would still look sexy." He chuckled, my face heating even more from his comment. "But as much as I would enjoy it, I would rather you wear clothes. Reservation is in an hour baby." He said huskily into my ear before slowly pulling out the pencil from my hair, watching as it tumbled down to my shoulders. He slowly ran his fingers against my scalp, massaging the ache away from the day. I closed my eyes as I let the moan escape my lips.

I felt his lips brush mine softly as I pulled his shirt into my clenched fists, basking in the innocence of the kiss. "Angel." I moaned against his lips, causing a growl to vibrate from his chest as he pulled away.

"Keep that up and we will never get out of here." He said breathlessly before running his thumb down my cheek. I leaned into his touch for mere seconds before he pulled away and lay down on my bed. His feet were crossed at his ankles as his arms stretched behind his head, wearing that sexy smirk that could make my panties wet and my knees weak.

All I could do was stand there not knowing how to make my brain work.

My God, this man could do crazy things to me even when he barely touches me.

"Tick, tock baby girl." He smiled, slowly shutting his eyes.

My brain finally kicked in after a few moments of staring at the 'sinful angel' on my bed, running to the closet I pulled out some black skinny jeans and a blue camisole. I wanted to look good for him, but given the time restraints, it would just have to do.

After about ten minutes of Angel reassuring me that I looked great, we finally made our way to the restaurant. It was only a twenty minute walk from campus. Angel didn't even bother bringing his car this time, which made me smile.

When we finally arrived at the restaurant, a tall and beautiful man was waiting at the entrance to greet us. He was a striking man with a sharp, broad jaw line and a beautiful tanned skin tone. My gaze reached his eyes, they were intense, but not in color. There was a fire behind them, a lot of fire. It suddenly dawned on me how much this man resembled Angel, were they related? His eyes were the complete polar opposite of Angel's. Angel's eyes were amazing shades of blue whereas this man's were a deep chocolate brown, they held so much warmth and they instantly made me feel at ease, but also completely off guard.

"Hey Uncle Mark, I didn't know you would be working tonight." Angel said as he pulled his uncle into a hug. I couldn't help but smile seeing that he had a good relationship with him, especially with the absence of his father. Well, that was until I saw Angel's lips were now pressed into a hard line when he pulled away from his uncles embrace, weird.

"I had to get some paper work that I left in the office." Mark explained as his eyes darted to me, looking me up and down as if he was trying to read me. "So, who is this little gem?" He still hadn't taken his eyes off me, I felt as though I was being interrogated with his chocolate eyes as they probed my body.

Was he…was he checking me out?

Angel hadn't made any move to introduce me, he just stood there with a hard expression on his face. I didn't understand what was going on but I needed to get his uncle to take his damn eyes off me!

"Hi, I'm Neva James." I said thrusting my hand out to Mark, desperately hoping that it would pull his eyes away from my body and look at my outstretched hand. He raised his right eyebrow before placing his hand in mine.

"Nice to meet you, Neva. I'm Mark Walker." He said as he shook my hand firmly. "Angel, can you help me move some of this paperwork?" He said as he snapped his head over to Angel who now looked so tense, it was unnerving.

"Sure." He said with a tight nod. "Take a seat at our table and I'll be right back."

He pointed to a table in the far corner of the room, the table was shielded by two large white pillars, giving us privacy from the rest of the restaurant.

"Okay, it was nice meeting you, Mark." I said before placing a swift kiss on Angel's cheek. I made my way to our table and took

139 • Finding You

a seat. I watched as Mark and Angel disappeared through a door at the far left of the room, weird.

What was all that about? It was weird enough the way Mark was looking at me, but it was just plain uncomfortable watching the strained exchange between uncle and nephew. I didn't have time to question it further as Angel suddenly appeared, taking his seat in front of me at the table. He looked as though he had just swallowed a sour lemon.

"Are you okay?" I asked, gently placing my hand on top of his that was resting on the table. His face screwed up into a scowl as he looked down at our hands, but before I could ask what was going on, he shook his head as if he was trying to rid it of his thoughts. A smile crept across his beautiful face as he gave my hand a reassuring squeeze.

"Yeah, I'm good now. I'm here with you."

The food was amazing. Angel ordered practically everything on the menu and insisted on feeding me small bites of everything. The tension that was in his shoulders seemed to have magically melted away, as if it was never there. His sexy smile was back as we enjoyed each other's company. We talked about music and college, like what happened before was no big deal. I couldn't help but notice that he avoided talking about his uncle.

My stomach was hurting from all the laughing we had been doing, although I suspect the amount of food I consumed was probably a factor too. I had to hold my stomach as we made our way back to my dorm.

"I had an awesome time tonight, Neva." He said as we walked up the campus staircase to the second floor, stopping in front of my dorm door on the narrow corridor.

"Me too." I smiled.

As I reached for my door, Angel suddenly spun me around in his arms, crashing his lips against mine, causing sensations to hit me like nothing before. I gasped, opening my mouth, his tongue glided against mine, pulling a moan from my lips. My hands found their way into his hair, fisting it at his scalp as I pulled him close to my body. My back quickly hit the door behind me as Angel guided me back. Suddenly, in one swift move, my legs were wrapped around his lean waist as he pressed his hardness between my legs. This wasn't sweet and romantic like before, this was hard and carnal, but it was laced with something I couldn't describe. I was lost in a sea of sensations as Angel's hands moved up my shirt, grazing his fingertips across my skin leaving scorch marks behind. He ground his hips into me while pinning me against the door. We moaned together as we basked in the touch of each other, treading new territory.

"I thought you would at least wait until you got in your room before you drop your panties, Neva. Real classy."

The voice alone made my head spin at an electrifying speed, making me dizzy with familiarity. Angel's head quickly snapped around to the source of the snide remark. I didn't need to look, I knew without a doubt who it was. Only one person could send my mind and body into a frenzy just by saying my name, Logan.

Without moving from our embrace Angel scowled at Logan, still keeping me pinned against the door while I tried to use Angel as a shield, but not from Logan. A shield from Angel himself, I didn't want him to see the effect Logan's voice alone did to my body.

"What did you just say, douchebag?" Angel spat, fury washed

over his face as he bore holes straight through Logan. I tried to untangle myself from Angel's body to try and stop the disaster that was happening right in front of me, but Angel was pinning me harder, causing my pelvis to ache.

"I thought you were better than that, Neva." Logan completely ignored what Angel had just said. He was just talking to me as if Angel wasn't even there. But Logan's words stung, tears filled my eyes as I watched Logan leave the corridor shaking his head. Suddenly I felt Angel's eyes on me, looking up, the fury was written all over his face.

"Who was that?" He said in thundering voice, I flinched in shock from the sheer anger that poured from him.

"Logan." I whimpered. My voice was shaky and my lips quivered as tears spilled down my cheeks. I was more afraid of Angel in this moment to even think to be upset over Logan's words.

"If I ever see him again or if he even tries to bad mouth you again, I will make him regret it." He said, his voice softer than before, but still firm enough to scare me.

"J...Just leave it Angel. He is my brother's best friend. He is probably wasted." I lied, tripping over my words at the sheer speed they fell out of my mouth trying to calm Angel down.

"I won't make any promises, Neva, but being wasted isn't an excuse to insult you." He said in a strained whisper as he rested his forehead against mine. He slowly ran his fingertips along my cheeks. I closed my eyes as he wiped away the tears that had escaped. "I'm sorry I scared you." He apologized, only inches from my lips.

"You didn't, I promise." I said pulling away from his touch, smiling weakly.

"Are you okay?" He searched my face for a hint of exactly what was going through my mind.

"I better go inside, it's late… I just need to get some sleep."

He pulled my face into his hands, running his fingertips down my cheeks. My body trembled under his touch.

"Are you sure you're okay?" He asked as he bent his knees, his eyes becoming eye level with mine.

"Yeah, I'm just tired." I said nodding, trying hard not to crack under his intense gaze.

His lips gently brushed against mine, taking me completely by surprise. It was so different from the kiss he gave me just moments ago, this man had so many different sides to him. Question is, can I keep up?

"Sweet dreams, baby." He said before walking down the corridor and out of the building, leaving me frozen on the spot.

*fourteen*

"You're going to Bones? Oh. My. God! I'm so jealous Nev." Low squealed. "And Angel knows Ryder Wilde? Damn, that boy could ride me any time!" She said, wiggling her eyebrows at me suggestively.

"Yeah, thanks for that mental image, Low." Does she always have to think with her vagina?

"What, you're telling me you wouldn't? You're in a relationship, Neva, not dead!"

"Okay, yes Ryder is hot. Now shut up and help me get ready, skank!"

"Ugh, you need to get laid soon. I am seriously considering sending you to a damn convent." Low chuckled at her own joke.

Rolling my eyes, I started rifling through our closet, what the hell do I wear to a rock bar?

"Come on baby girl, Low is driving me crazy out here!" Tate shouted from outside the bathroom door an hour later. "Ouch!

Jesus baby! What was that for?"

"For being an ass." I heard Low reply. I couldn't help but chuckle and shake my head at my brother and best friend.

"Okay you bunch of kids, I'm coming!" I said, placing my other matching earring in before opening the door and walking out into the room.

"God damn, I'm good!" Low grinned, admiring her handy work.

Low had helped me pick out my outfit, a snug fitting black Jack Daniels vest top, coupled with tight, low slung jeans. My hair was thrown up in a messy ponytail, slightly curled at the ends. My make-up was dramatic. My eyes accentuating my outfit with a smoky effect, my lips were lined with a bright scarlet red. Teamed with my black leather jacket and Converse, I was ready to go.

"Jesus Neva, you look awesome!" Tate said, flashing me a smile. I think he was more enthusiastic than I was.

"Thanks Tate, so what's this rock bar like then?" I asked, turning to Low. I was curious to know what I was about to walk into.

"Rock bar?" She said, looking at me confused.

"Uh yeah, what should I expect?" I said, furrowing my brows at the look of utter confusion on Low's face.

"Neva, Bones isn't a rock bar, sweetie." She said with a chuckle. "It's a biker bar."

"A what?" Tate and I shrieked at the same time, what the hell?

"Are you kidding, Low? You better be fucking around." Tate said, clearly not happy at Low's little revelation.

"Baby she will be fine." Low said to Tate before turning back to me. "Do you want me to go with you?" She asked. I didn't know if she wanted to go to watch out for me or because she wanted to get a glimpse of Ryder.

"No, I'm good. I'm sure I will be fine." I said, trying to reassure myself more than anybody else.

"If you get uncomfortable or just want to come home, you can call me or Logan. Okay?" Tate said, placing his hands on my shoulders, squeezing gently.

"Okay." I nodded.

"Let's get our asses on the road then!" Tate said, making our way down to his truck.

"You sure about this?" Tate asked as we pulled into the parking lot, eying up the endless rows of motorcycles lining the outside of the bar.

"Tate I will be fine, I'll be with Angel." I said, sending Angel a quick text, letting him know I was outside.

"Speaking of Angel, where is he?" He asked. "I need to make sure he is going to look after my baby girl." His brow furrowed quickly as he focused on the entrance of the bar.

I turned my gaze to where Tate was staring wide-eyed, watching as a figure emerged from the darkness.

"He's here." I smiled, my mouth parting as I salivated from the sight before me. Tight ripped jeans hugged muscular thighs as he walked, a black vest top showcased broad shoulders and strong, masculine forearms. But my eyes locked on a black and white bandanna that hung loosely around his neck, damn he was sexy!

"*That's* Angel?" Tate asked, throwing his gaze back to me, the worry evident on his face.

"Oh, yeah." I said smiling. "Come and meet him, he won't bite, Tate." I said over my shoulder as I got out of the truck, Tate slowly following me.

"Jesus baby, you look so fucking sexy." Angel growled into my ear as he wrapped his arms around my waist, kissing me gently behind the shell of my ear.

"Angel, this is my brother, Tate." I said, pulling out of Angel's arms. "Tate, this is Angel."

I watched as they eyed each other suspiciously, waiting for one of them to react.

"I will only warn you once, watch out for her or I will make sure the football team use you as a replacement for the punch bags." Tate said, tight lipped.

Holy shit! Did he really just say that?

"Tate!" I spat, glaring at my brother for being so damn rude.

"No, it's okay Neva." Angel said, setting towards Tate. "I will make sure your sister is safe, you have my word."

Tate nodded once, seemingly happy with Angel's response. Turning to me he placed a kiss on my cheek.

"Call me if you need me, baby girl." He said, before getting in his truck and speeding off.

"You ready, baby?" Angel asked, his eyes raking my body as his gaze scorched my skin.

I nodded, my hand tingling as his fingers entwined with mine. Pulling my hand to his lips before slowly running his tongue across my knuckles, shit that was...Wow!

Angel led me through to the darkened entrance of the bar, rock music poured through the door that stood in front of us.

My heartbeat synchronized with the thundering base. Through the shadows I saw Angel's eyes brighten, his smile visible as we finally came out from the blanket of darkness and into a dimly lit bar.

"You want a drink?" Angel asked as we made our way over to the bar, my eyes adjusting to the scene before me.

"Sure." I said nervously, shifting from one foot to the other.

"Dex!" Angel shouted. A tall man with dark hair and green eyes turned from behind the bar, smiling as he spotted Angel.

"It's been a long time, man, where the fuck have you been hiding?" Dex said as he made his way over to us. His voice was husky and warm, like melted sex.

"I know, man. I brought my girl for the open mic night." Angel said, flicking his eyes to me.

"So, this is where you have been hiding?" Dex said, a smile creeping across his face, instantly making me feel at ease. "I'm Dex, your gorgeous bartender for the night." He said with a wink, Angel laughed at his friend's forwardness.

"I'm Neva." I said, checking out the mass of tattoos that adorned Dex's arms as he leaned on to the bar.

"Nice to meet you, Neva." He said before turning to Angel. "Usual?"

Angel nodded while Dex pushed two bottles of beer down the bar towards us. Picking up his beer, Angel slapped a twenty on the bar before thanking Dex.

"You going up there tonight, dude?" Dex asked with an eyebrow raised.

"Yeah, I have a little something up my sleeve for tonight though. Save me a spot will ya?" Angel said over his shoulder as we walked towards a table near the small stage.

As we took our seats, my eyes darted around the room, taking in the mass of people crammed into one space. The walls were dated, a mixture of black and white matching the tiled floor. Electric guitars lined the wall near the stage, and pictures of motorcycles were dotted around the room.

"Dude, you got the first spot, man. You're up in ten." Dex said, leaning in between Angel and I. "Betty is round the back," Dex said with a smirk before wandering off into the sea of people. "Make way! Sexy ass motherfucker coming through!" I heard him shout before disappearing from sight.

"He is a unique one." Angel growled into my ear, the heat of his breath sending chills down my spine. "Are you ready, baby?" He asked, his lips grazing my ear.

"Ready for what?" I whispered hoarsely, damn he could make me melt instantly!

"Come with me," he said, placing his hand around my wrist, leading me through a door, which I presumed led into the back of the bar.

We walked into a small room filled with bottles and mixers. I didn't even realize there were that many different types of alcohol. In a darkened corner, I noticed an acoustic with the name 'Betty Black' inscribed into the body, turning to Angel, I giggled.

"Betty Black? I thought you said it was just called Betty." I said raising my brow. Angel chuckled as he ran his hand through his hair.

"She was...I decided if I was going to look like a complete and utter cock then I had better do it in style." He said with a shrug, but that was when I noticed it. Another acoustic sitting next to it...my acoustic.

My father's acoustic.

I quickly turned to look at Angel, what the fuck? Why was my acoustic here? I was just about ready to rip him a new one when his lips suddenly crashed against mine. His tongue quickly sought mine as his arms wrapped around my waist, pulling me closer. His kiss was making my head spin, he tasted of beer and that unique taste that was Angel Walker.

"Don't freak out." He murmured against my lips. "I thought it was time that you shared your pain. You won't see these people again. It is a room full of strangers that are going to get really drunk and probably not even remember you singing." His lips lightly grazed against mine before he continued. "I want you to try and release some of your pain, let them take some of the weight from your shoulders Neva. You don't have to carry all of it on your own." Angel's forehead rested against mine as he sighed a heavy breath, clearly nervous of my reaction. Did I want to do this? I mean, Angel had a point, I wasn't going to see them again and what would it hurt? They won't remember it.

"Okay." I agreed, shocking Angel and myself.

"Okay." He repeated back, feeling him smile against my lips as he tenderly kissed me.

*fifteen*

MY HANDS SHOOK AS I FELT MY spine become slick with sweat, my eyes darting out across the room to the unsuspecting bikers drinking and laughing. They had no idea about the mental breakdown I was having right there on the stage, why did I think this was a good idea again? Oh yeah, that's right. Angel kissed me until I was dizzy enough to yes to anything. I am going to kill him after this.

"Don't worry baby, I am with you every step of the way." Angel said into my ear, standing at my side as he placed my acoustic over my head, the strap resting on my shoulder.

"I'm going to kill you later." I whisper-shouted back at him.

"You can do anything you like to me later, baby." Angel winked.

Angel swiftly placed his guitar over his shoulder. Shit, I was nervous. The microphone inches away from my face, I was sure I could hear my staggered breathing over the speakers.

What the fuck am I doing? I turned, ready to walk off the stage when I felt a hand on my shoulder.

"You can do this." Angel said from behind me, his voice penetrating my thoughts of running. "Come on baby, I will be right with you." His hand squeezed my shoulder before turning me towards him.

"I don't think I can, I don't...I don't know if I can do this, Angel." My voice trailed off, this was my worst nightmare coming to life. These people were going to hear my voice, my pain and I didn't know if I was ever going to be ready to bare my soul, my weaknesses.

"Baby, you can do this. You were born to sing, Neva. Your voice can bring life to the lifeless, love to the loveless and maybe even mend a broken heart. If you can't do this for you, do it for me. Sing life back into me. Bring me back from my lifeless existence." Angel pleaded, his eyes glazing over with unshed tears. That one confession had completely broken me. Angel thought he was leading a lifeless existence but he didn't know that he was slowly mending my broken heart. I could do it for him. I could give him life as he had given me a reason to mend.

"For you." I whispered, placing a gentle kiss onto his cheek, lingering as his leaned into my lips, closing his eyes.

"Thank you."

"Do you know what you want to play?" He asked with a smile.

I stopped for a moment to think about what I could sing that would help Angel, help me. An idea came to mind but I wasn't going to tell him what I was going to play, this was for him.

"Just follow my lead." I said, mustering the little confidence that I had left.

My fingers strummed against the strings on my acoustic, pulling the familiar tune that I had played so many times before. As the lyrics of "Bound to You" by Christina Aguilera left my mouth, I heard a gasp from behind me, my voice carrying over the speakers making some of the audience turn to face me. I can do this I told myself, it was time to pass on some of my pain.

The song seemed so appropriate. I knew I was in a biker bar, but I needed to make my feelings clear, I am broken but I now had a reason to mend. I scanned the crowd as I sung, watching as more and more people turned towards me, seemingly interested in the timid girl playing a love song in a biker bar.

I had just moved into the second chorus when I noticed someone walking into the bar, my eyes widened when I realized it was Logan. He stood on the spot, seemingly frozen in place from the sound of my voice. I watched as he closed his eyes; I pushed myself through the rest of the song as tears stung my eyes. My mind became a foggy mess, reminding me that I was broken and I may never heal. My pain would hurt everyone around me my mom, my brother, Logan...Angel.

My voice suddenly became shaky as I tried to wrap my tongue around the lyrics, lyrics that held so much pain and meaning, twisting the knife deeper and penetrating every single piece of me. Closing my eyes, I concentrated on the last lines of the song, pushing all the pain to the tip of my tongue, ready to try and release it.

'I am bound to you...'

A single tear rolled down my cheek as I glanced at Logan, still frozen on the spot. His eyes wide, glossed over with unshed tears as if feeling my pain, taking it and keeping it...protecting me from it. I didn't notice the clapping or the cheers from the audience nor did I hear Angel call my name, but I noticed Logan's brows furrowing and a frown pulling at his lips, seemingly confused by something.

A hand on my shoulder made me flinch slightly, as if pulling me out of a world where there was only Logan and me.

"Baby, that was...amazing." Angel praised, his body pressed into my back. The evidence of what my voice must have done to him pressed into the back of my right thigh.

"Thank you." I said softly, reluctantly turning around to face him. My body wanted to stay where it was as my eyes moved away from Logan, my breathing slowed from the peace I felt from singing, but a sense of unease washed over me....Who had I just sang that song for? For me? For Angel? Or for Logan?

*sixteen*

"If you're not careful, your tits will spill out of that." I said, pointing at Low's ridiculously revealing dress as we got ready for another one of Ace's parties.

"It's not my fault I have a great rack." She said chuckling.

Rolling my eyes, I turned towards the mirror as I applied a coat of gloss to my lips, quickly glancing over at my chosen outfit. I had picked a gorgeous red dress that stopped just above the knee. It was tight in all the right places, showing off my curvy figure. My hair was loose against my back as it curled at the tips, but it was my legs that stood out the most. They looked even longer than before, thanks to my sky-high black heels.

It was now Friday night, four days since I bared my feelings and weaknesses to a biker bar. I was still unsure what came over me to sing that particular song, and just who I was singing it to. I hadn't seen Logan since that night and I couldn't tell anyone about what happened, not even Low, who had been acting really weird recently. Any time I mentioned my brother, she would give me a smile that said, 'I'm forcing this' or just avoid the subject completely.

"Are you and Tate okay?" I asked tentatively, not knowing how she was going to react. Maybe they haven't made up over the argument yet.

"Uh yeah, fine." She shrugged as she turned her back to me, placing her tiny feet into her heels. That was a sure sign she wasn't going to elaborate further. Something wasn't right, I didn't know what it was but something was telling me it wasn't good.

"Okay." I said placing my phone into the cup of my bra. "Angel is meeting us at Ace's." I said as we made our way out of the dorm room and down the street to the party.

Ace's house came in to view as we turned the corner just off campus, the music blaring so loud that even people as far away as Canada could hear it. It wasn't as packed as the last party, but there were enough people there to make it hard to get through the door without one body part touching another.

Low and I walked down the hallway towards the large kitchen, skirting around couples dry humping each other against any hard surface they could find. Walking in I looked around to see if I could spot Angel, but he was nowhere in sight. Pulling out my phone, I sent him a text to let him know I was here waiting for him.

Placing the phone back into my bra, I made my way over to the corner of the room where Tate, Ace, Zane and Colt stood laughing and joking. I watched as Low bounced over to my brother, placing a chaste kiss on his mouth. Huh? Weird, I thought they were fighting? Then I noticed it and I gasped in shock, Tate's eye was ten shades of black and blue. Walking over to him, I pulled him by his wrist, dragging him to a quiet spot in the back yard.

"What the hell is that?" I spat as I pointed at his eye, it was one hell of a black eye.

"It's a black eye, sis." He said nonchalantly as he pushed my finger away from his face, chuckling.

Did he think this was some kind of joke?

"I know what it is, Tate, but how the hell did you get it?" I asked as I crossed my arms over my chest, becoming increasingly concerned.

Is this why Low had been so jumpy every time I mentioned my brother? I could feel the wheels spinning round in my head but the only conclusion I could come up with was Low. Had she done this? I could feel my blood boiling. What the fuck?

"I was tackled on the field, it's no big deal. I'm fine." He said smiling as he pulled me in for a hug. "I'm fine, I promise." I should feel reassured that he got it from the football field and that he was okay. But I wasn't, he is my brother. I have seen him happy, sad, excited and depressed; but I have also seen him lie and right now, he was lying.

I remember when I was around seven, mom had made her famous triple chocolate sponge cake for dad's birthday. It was three layers of a heart attack waiting to happen but my God, mom's baking was incredible. Mom had gone upstairs to get changed out of her flour-coated clothes, leaving the cake on the table in the dining room. Yeah, you know what's coming next right? Tate took the biggest portion I had ever seen and ate every last bit. Even with chocolate crumbs around his mouth he still lied through his back teeth. He even had the nerve to tell mom it was all my idea! Of course, we were both sent to our rooms.

Since then, Tate had mastered the white lie but he could never fool me, his eyes were the biggest tell. They would widen ever so slightly. To anyone else, this would have gone unnoticed; but not to me.

I quickly pulled out of his arms. Why was he lying? What isn't he telling me?

"Don't lie to me, Tate Michael James! What really happened?"

"Logan happened." Whipping my head around, I watched as a scowl appeared on Low's face as she walked over to Tate and straight into his open arms, holding her close. "Look, Tate didn't want me to tell you, but I knew your mind would go into overdrive once you saw that he was lying to you." Low shrugged while looking at the ground.

"Why didn't you want to tell me, Tate?" I asked, my heartbeat rising. Shit, he knows about Logan.

"I knew you would be mad at him. He was pissed when he got back to the dorm, Nev. I asked him to go to Bones and watch over you. He came back home and he looked pissed. And when I asked him what the hell was going on, he went on a rampage! The dorm was completely turned upside down. The damn walls have holes in them, and when I tried to calm him down, he swung for me."

"Where is he?" I shot, cutting him off, still trying to take in what Tate had just told me.

"Back at the dorm." Quickly turning, I made my way out of the house as Tate shouted over my shoulder "Be careful, Neva."

My heels clacked and scraped against the tarmac of the road

as I ran full speed towards campus. I was going to either land on my face or break my neck from the damn things. I quickly kicked off my heels, leaving them on the side of the road. I didn't care, they weren't important. What was important was that Logan was hurting and it was my fault.

I felt ten years old again. My chest heaved and my lungs hurt from the quick breaths I was taking as I sprinted down the road. My eyes watered, blurring my vision as the wind whipped my face while my head hurt with the internal battle I was facing. Should I be running to him? Should I be dropping everything for him? He has hurt me time and time again, but right now I don't think my brain could come up with a rational answer. I needed to get to him.

Pain shot through the soles of my bare feet as they pounded against the campus grounds. I could feel gravel clinging to my feet as it tore small cuts across the sensitive skin. I was suddenly aware of my fist hammering against a solid surface. It took me a few moments to realize I was outside Tate and Logan's dorm. I couldn't remember getting into the building or climbing the stairs to the corridor where I now stood.

"Open the door, Logan!" I shouted while ramming my fist into the wood, feeling my hand splinter in pain from the sheer force I was pushing through my body into my fist. My hand stopped mid-air before I could do anymore damage to both my hand and the door. I heard the sound of a bottle hitting the floor followed by a muffled 'shit'. Placing my ear against the door I tried to make out any more sounds or movement from the other side, but I was met with silence.

"You better open this damn door, Logan White, or I swear

I'll…" My mouth quickly snapped shut as I was suddenly eye level with a very toned, a very naked and a very sexy chest. Rock solid pecs greeted me as his lower torso invited me to look down. Abs that were perfectly defined in impeccable mounds that left my mouth watering, flexed under my gaze. But my eyes were uncontrollable as they roamed further down to that damn sexy 'V'. Visions of licking and biting that spot flooded my mind.

"Or you'll what?" The growl in Logan's voice didn't go unnoticed as I pried my ogling eyes from his God-like body, finally locking my gaze on his face, trying hard not to look back down again. But I was quickly taken aback when I saw Logan's blood-shot eyes.

"You're drunk." I said as I pushed past him, causing him to stumble slightly as I walked into the room. My eyes roamed around to find any trace of evidence of Logan's 'rampage' but everything looked the way it should, well except from the fist-size hole in the wall just above his bed.

My feet suddenly started to ache in pain as the adrenaline left my body. Christ it was painful. My knees started to buckle from under me. I quickly sat down on the edge of Logan's bed, giving me a little relief as I took the weight off my now swollen and blood tinged feet. Looking down, I cringed. This was going to really hurt in the morning!

I was suddenly aware of a hand on my ankle. Logan's strong hands were grasping at my foot as he crouched down on the floor in front of me. Raising my foot higher to investigate the sole, I watched him carefully as I saw his brows furrow clearly confused as to why I had no shoes on.

"We need to clean these up." He said, his eyes never left my foot as he said those words to me. Then it hit me.

"No Logan, I'm fine." I didn't want him doing this. I didn't even think about it when I took my damn shoes off. Logan hated the sight of blood.

"If you're worried I am going to faint on you, don't. I haven't done that since I was fifteen."

The memory of Logan fainting on the floor in our back yard made me chuckle. Tate had broken his arm when he fell out of the old oak tree. He was showing off, trying to climb to the top telling us all that he was the best tree climber. But he didn't make it past the fourth branch, falling on his right arm he screamed out from the pain. I'm not surprised he screamed and cried as much as he did. He had hurt his arm pretty bad. Mom came running outside to see what was going on, pulling Tate to sit up against the tree, his injury was pretty evident. Bone was sticking out of his arm while blood poured profusely from it. I sat down next to him to comfort him when I noticed Logan's face paling. His large frame suddenly hit the deck with a thud, he had fainted. Tate needed surgery to fix his arm, but made a full recovery. As for Logan? He didn't live it down for weeks from Tate and me.

Logan's hands left my ankle as he stood up and walked into his bathroom, leaving my skin hot just from the most innocent of touch. Shit, this wasn't a good idea. I quickly stood up, causing pain to shoot through my feet, making my legs weak. I need to get out of here.

"Neva, sit down before you fall on your damn face."

Logan's arms wrapped around my waist as he gently guided me back down on the bed, crouching back down on the floor and producing a damp towel. Slowly, he wiped away the blood from my feet, never taking his eyes off the task at hand. I watched him closely, watching for any sign of him becoming faint. The last thing I needed was him face-planting on the floor.

Logan took his time, ensuring he got every last bit of blood and dirt from my feet. The meticulously slow, even strokes were damn near hypnotic. I closed my eyes and allowed my body just to feel how the towel brushed against my skin so gently. Logan's breath grazed against my skin as he concentrated on cleaning my feet. He slowly moved from one foot to the other. His eyes still fixed on the lower half of my body, still not looking up at me. But when I looked down at him once again, I was met with Logan's gorgeous brown eyes staring up at me. His hand trailed from my ankle to my calf, massaging my sore muscles that burned from the run that brought me here.

"What are you…"

"Don't talk, Neva, just listen." He sighed as his hands rubbed the knots out of my muscles, pampering my skin.

"You have been driving me crazy since we were kids. With your cute little button nose that scrunched up when you were confused, or the way you used to take fries from my damn plate even though you said you weren't hungry. Even when you used to cry when you watched Bambi. But now, you drive me crazy in other ways. The way your button nose now scrunches up when you smile. It's no longer cute, it's sexy. The way you now pick up one of my fries and feed it to me before taking one for yourself, which isn't freaking annoying anymore. It's hot. The way you still cry at Bambi, but now try and hide your face with your hair when you do it. It makes me want to hold you and brush your hair out of your beautiful face."

If I was standing up, his words would have knocked me off my feet. Taking a deep breath, he carried on.

"Do you know what the best part is, Neva?" I couldn't form words, I shook my head in response.

"You have no idea that I have been in love with you from the moment I held you for the first time. When you were just ten years old."

My world stopped and my head spun, did he just say love?

"I don't understand, I…" Logan's fingertip softly grazed my lips, stopping me from continuing.

"See, all I can think about is that kiss. I can see it in my dreams, I can taste it every time I touch my lips and I can feel it every time I close my eyes. But seeing you with Angel tears me apart, Nev. It fucking shatters me." I couldn't take my eyes off him as his words sunk in, rendering me mute.

"But I know I will never be good enough for you, you deserve so much better than me. You told me to leave you alone and I've tried. Fuck, I have tried, Neva. But every time I try, I get this ache in my chest and it hurts, it hurts so fucking much."

"Logan, I…" I didn't know what to say, what do you say to the man who you love but are too scared to tell? Scared that one day he could be taken away from me in a blink of an eye. Scared that he could crush my heart further. Realization suddenly consumed me, I loved him.

"I'm with Angel." The words tumbled out of my mouth on a choked sob. "And you, you're with…"

"No, Neva, I'm not. We aren't together."

"But you said…"

"No, I didn't. You saw me with Georgia and you assumed

we were together. We never have been together. She was a stand in, a distraction. They have all been a damn distraction from the one woman I could never have. The one woman I didn't deserve." Tears stung my eyes as his words hit me full force like a slap in the face.

He wasn't with Georgia, but it didn't change anything. I am with Angel and I really like him. He doesn't know about my demons and what happened to my family and I liked that. I didn't have to explain it. It kept me safe.

"I'm with Angel." I repeated. I didn't know if I was trying to convince Logan or myself. But this was the only way I could protect myself. I desperately wanted to tell Logan that I was in love with him. But I knew that if I did, I would open myself up for more heartbreak. So I did the only thing I knew how, I pushed him away.

"I'm sorry, Logan." I watched as a stray tear gently rolled down his cheekbone, silently shattering me further.

"I know." His voice broke against the sobs that were desperate to escape.

I couldn't look at him, just watching that single tear roll down his cheek was enough torture for me to endure. I quickly stood and made my way to the door, stepping over Logan in the process. Reaching out for the doorknob I grasped it in my hand tightly, turning my knuckles white from my grasp.

"Don't leave me, Neva." The whispered sobs tumbled into my ear as Logan's body enclosed around mine, keeping me from running.

"I have to." I had to close my eyes to stop the tears that threatened to escape just from the pleading in his voice. The overwhelming urge to hold him, sooth him, love him was becoming too much to bare.

"Give me one last taste, give me that. Please."

I didn't have time to think, never mind respond, before Logan had twisted me in his arms. He swiftly pinned my body against the door that I was ready to walk out of just moments before. Seconds passed as he stared into my eyes, searching for something. I knew he found what he was looking for when his lips suddenly collided against mine, sending fireworks through my body like the 4th of July, pushing every nerve, every muscle, and every heartbeat into an explosive frenzy. I shouldn't kiss him, but my desire for Logan outweighed any conscious thought that my mind could produce.

Our lips were locked in an innocent embrace, neither of us taking the kiss further. Both unsure of the others possible reaction, but need pooled somewhere deep inside me. My body burned and screamed 'give it to him'.

So, I did.

A moan escaped my lips as Logan's scent invaded my senses, spiced apple and cinnamon clouded my body and judgment. My lips parted as I tentatively ran my tongue across Logan's perfectly defined bottom lip, tasting the saltiness of his tears. Collecting them, savoring them.

My hand trailed up to his muscular neck, entwining my fingers through the tips of his unbelievably soft hair as Logan deepened the kiss. He probed my tongue with his, expertly taking me, exploring me. This was no longer innocent. This was hot and frantic, and my body was responding shamelessly as I groaned from the sudden change of direction as our bodies became one.

"Oh shit." Logan muttered against my mouth as he took hold of my exposed thighs, wrapping my legs around his waist. His fingers dug into my flesh as I moaned from the intense sensation of his hardness against my core. Only my lace panties and his dark denim jeans separated us. But holy shit, it felt so good.

I couldn't think, I couldn't breathe. All I could do was feel as Logan's hips pinned me against the door while his tongue frantically searched my mouth, was him taking every last piece of me.

"Logan." I moaned as he ground his hips against my core, sending electricity throughout my whole damn body. It fueled my need and desire for more. So much more. Just a whisper of his name and he was growling against my mouth. We were so close as our bodies entwined at the most intimate points. Logan quickly found a slow, torturous rhythm as he ground his hips into my core. My eyes rolled as I threw my head back against the door, moaning as Logan's teeth quickly found my neck. Grazing my skin, he slowly pushed me further to the edge.

My nails scraped against his scalp while his hips ground against me over and over, again. I was panting and breathless as he swiftly encircled my wrists with both hands, quickly pinning them above my head. His hair stroked my hypersensitive skin as his head rested in the crook of my neck once more. He was licking, biting, and sucking while he increased the pressure in his hips.

"Please." I panted, I had no idea what I was pleading for. For him to stop? To carry on?

Oh God, carry on...

My mind was running at lightning speed when Logan

took my earlobe between his teeth, my whole body started to buck underneath his. My body twisted into a ball of desire that was desperate to release. Everything scorched and burned simultaneously as Logan ground his hips into mine one last time, before he whispered into my ear.

"I love you."

The moan that erupted from my throat was hoarse and husky as my body found its release. He swallowed my scream with a sensually slow kiss, prolonging the earth-shattering pleasure that had completely consumed me.

## seventeen

"I'M SORRY." I SAID AGAINST Logan's chest, my breathing came back down to a reasonable level for me to actually produce words. But I quickly regretted them as soon as they tumbled from my mouth when Logan quickly pulled back from me.

"What are you sorry for?" He asked gently, taking my face in his hands. He ran the pads of his thumbs over my skin, sending a rush of tingles through my now limp body.

"For me, I...Er."

"Neva? Was that your first orgasm?" The look on Logan's face didn't give anything away. What would he think if he knew that he just took another piece of me?

"Neva, please answer me." He pleaded. I couldn't get the words out of my mouth. The only thing I could do was nod and close my eyes, not wanting to see his reaction.

"Damn." He mumbled before taking my lips against his,

kissing me like I had never been kissed before. It was so soft and sweet, making my heart flutter, my knees weak and my head dizzy.

"Stay with me." He asked against my lips, my head was all over the place. Logan and I had shared a bed many times before, usually when he had to pull me out from one of my nightmares. But things are different now, we are different now.

"Logan, I can't." I pleaded. I needed him to stop. I needed this to stop. I was only so strong.

"Neva, if I can't touch you, feel you or kiss you ever again after tonight, then I want you to stay with me. We will just sleep I promise."

Things had already gone too far tonight, a line had been crossed and there was no going back for either of us. But the thought of falling asleep in Logan's arms one last time was making my heart ache. I needed Logan to soothe that ache. Even if it was just for one night.

"Okay."

I know I shouldn't be doing this, but it was him. It has always been him. My Logan.

"Thank you."

He pressed his lips against my neck softly before carrying me over to his bed, gently laying me down on his pillow and crawled up my body. He ran his hands down my ribs before reaching around to my back, lifting me slightly so my back curved and arched from the bed as he found the zipper of my dress. I searched his eyes frantically, trying to understand what he was doing.

"Relax." He smiled as he slowly pulled down the zipper,

releasing me of the confines of my tight clothes. My dress was now completely unzipped and just resting against my skin when Logan's hands left my body as he sat back, sighing.

"What's wrong?" I asked, nervous that he might having second thoughts.

"I don't want anything between us tonight Neva, but I don't know if I have enough restraint not to take you and make you mine." His fingers trailed a line from my jaw to ribs.

Oh. God.

"I want to feel you."

His hands reached my ribs and had started running lazy circles over my dress, a moan escaping my lips as his fingertips grazed my bare skin at the back of my dress.

"To know you."

He suddenly moved from my ribs to my temple, placing his palm against my cheek. Leaning into his touch, I closed my eyes. His strong hands cradled my face.

"To own you."

His hands wrapped around my face as he leant his forehead against mine, sneaking the softest of kisses from my lips.

"But right now, I want to make love to you. Let me in Neva, let me love you." I gasped, this man could undo me like no other, but was I ready to give him that piece of me? A piece of me that no one else could ever take?

"I don't know if I can."

Could I let him in, knowing that I would be more vulnerable than ever before?

"I don't think my heart could take it if I can't love you right now." He pleaded, as he rained kisses all over my face from my eyes, to my cheeks to my nose.

"I don't know how." I confessed as he pressed a soft butterfly kiss on the corner of my mouth, drawing out a moan. I lay there desperately wondering if he understood the double meaning of my words.

"Then let me show you."

I gasped. I didn't want anything between us either and it was time I faced the facts. I loved this man deeply and if I couldn't tell him with words, I was just going to have to show him. Sitting up, I quickly grasped at the hem of my dress as I slowly peeled it away from my body and over my head. I could hear a whispered gasp escape Logan's lips as I threw my dress on the floor. I was exposed in only my black bra and matching lace panties, but I didn't feel vulnerable. I felt empowered from the way Logan was watching me closely, taking in every single inch of my body.

Feeling confident, I took hold of Logan's neck with both hands, pulling us both back down to the bed. His forehead rested against mine as he looked straight into my eyes. I watched as he tried desperately not to look down at my body once more.

With his hands on both sides of my head and his knees in between my thighs, he was holding his weight off of me. I wanted him close with no barriers. I wanted Logan's bare chest against mine. To shield me, to hold me, to love me. Placing my still sore feet against the top of his knees I pushed hard against them, sending Logan's body crashing against mine.

"Shit." He groaned.

The sudden change in pressure as our bodies collided sent my mind spiraling into overdrive while my body splintered into a hole, filled with pleasure, desire and need.

"Neva." He groaned as he rested his weight against my body. His hips flush to my aching core as his breath grazed my skin causing my whole body to shudder underneath his weight.

"I want you so fucking bad." He growled huskily into my ear, fueling the raging fire that was already burning deep in my belly. Taking my earlobe between his teeth once more he sucked and licked gently, sending any rational thought straight out of the window.

"When I take you Neva, I am going to make damn sure you will never forget it."

The husk in his voice was turning me into putty in his hands, ready to be molded.

I was suddenly aware of his hands around my waist as he quickly shifted our bodies, pulling me onto his lap. I wrapped my legs around his defined torso, my arms around his neck. We were nose to nose as he trailed his hand down to my bra. His deft fingers making short work of the clasp as he slowly peeled the straps from my shoulders, exposing me. His eyes never left mine as he threw my bra across the room, turning me on even more.

"I'm too scared to look Neva." He whispered, closing his eyes. "Scared that I will wake up and this will all be just a dream."

The insecurity in his voice fueled me further. This was just as scary for me as it was for him. This was new territory and we were both about to go into battle.

"It's not a dream." I reassured as I pulled his hand from my waist guiding it up to my exposed breast. He groaned as his fingertips swept across my aching nipple. Logan's eyes flew wide open before quickly looking down to find his hand covering my breast. Suddenly he grabbed me at my waist and guided me down on my back, plunging his mouth around my nipple.

Taking my aching peak between his teeth he nibbled playfully as my hands found his hair, grasping at the roots and balling it into fists. I moaned from the new sensations taking over my body. My eyes rolled and my core ached as Logan lapped at my nipple, causing it to peak against his skillful tongue. He took his time worshiping my peak before showing the same attention to the other, nibbling, sucking and licking me into a damn frenzy. I couldn't see straight. The fire in my belly was becoming an inferno, past the point of stopping.

"Logan, please." I begged, moaning as he bit down hard on my nipple. I felt his hand trailing down to my now soaking panties.

"Shh, I've got you baby. I always have." A sudden jolt of electricity surged through my veins as Logan's fingers glided against my wet folds. "I always will."

His expert fingers found their way to my swollen clit as he rained kisses across the swell of my breasts. Slowly making his way up my neck and biting playfully across my jaw he gently kissed the corner of my mouth.

"Always." He captured my mouth with his as he slowly slid a finger inside me. Moaning, I quickly adjusted to the new sensations. Logan's tongue slowly danced with mine while he gently drew his finger from inside me, only to push back in at a slightly different angle. My vision blurred from the sensory overload. It wasn't fast and frantic anymore. This was love. This was Logan making love to me.

"No more barriers." He said as he pulled his hand away from the inside of my panties. I couldn't help but moan in protest. I started whimpering while I watched as Logan took my panties with his teeth. As he slowly pulled them down my legs, he trailed his hands down the inside of my thighs following in the path of my panties.

Once my panties hit the floor, all I could do was watch as Logan hurriedly unsnapped his jeans, taking them off with lightning speed, leaving him kneeling there in all his glory. Holy hot damn! The man doesn't wear boxers! His cock was standing proud and unashamed, making my mouth water with anticipation.

"Don't look so scared, Neva. I will take care of you. Take care of us." He said, clearly sensing my fear. Swiftly rolling on a condom, he crawled up my body once more. Placing his hands on either side of my head, he slowly lowered his body against mine, holding himself just mere inches away from me.

"I love you Neva James. Forever." His breath tickled my lips as I felt the sudden intrusion of Logan inside me. A sudden pinch, a bite, then sweet and unfaltering pleasure as Logan stripped away the last of the barriers between us.

"I will always love you." He pleaded, looking straight into my eyes.

"Oh God."

"I will always protect you."

We found our own sweet rhythm as he slid out of me before sliding back in at a faster pace. Stars danced in front of my eyes as the inferno of fire inside of me started to spread.

"I will always keep you safe."

His words were penetrating my heart and my mind as the fire became wild and unforgiving, burning at scorching temperatures. The only thing I could do was let it burn.

"Logan."

I couldn't form words. Nothing I could say would come close to anything I felt for this man. This man who had taken every single piece of me, my fears, my demons, my heart and soul. And now my virginity.

"You will always have my heart."

Tears stung my eyes as the familiar knot awakened deep inside me, my hands quickly wrapped around Logan's neck as I pulled him close. I needed his lips on mine, I needed him to know.

Our lips collided as his hips moved in a sexy, slow tempo sending my mind, body and soul to the edge. Our tongues danced frantically as I put everything I felt into that one kiss, hoping he understood exactly how I felt. That I loved him, so much.

My whole body was ablaze as Logan changed the angle of his hips so quickly that I screamed out his name. He was unrelenting as my moans of pleasure entwined with his groans of desire.

"I'll spend the rest of my life loving you. I will always love you, Neva." He said, before plunging inside me once more as the inferno detonated inside me. He took me to a place that I couldn't comprehend, splitting me in half with an orgasm so fierce it took my breath away.

"I love you."

The walls inside me contracted from the incredible tingling that encased my body from just his words, as Logan's hips jerked and his back bowed.

"I fucking love you." He groaned as he found his own release.

It was right then, in that moment that I realized that Logan

White had captured my heart. I could only hope that he wouldn't break it.

*eighteen*

I WAS HOT, SO FREAKING HOT. All I could feel was heat, why was I so damn warm? I slowly pried my eyes open, smiling when I noticed Logan sound asleep. His right arm was resting above his head as he slept on his back, he looked so peaceful. His gorgeous features even more pronounced in the morning light as he slept. He was stunning.

His arm was underneath me, cradling my body, while his leg was slung over my waist, trapping me, keeping me. I needed to make this as painless as possible, for him. Not for me, I deserved to feel like shit; to be the bad person. My heart will break, it will shatter, but surely it would be worse if we were together. My demons and fears would tear us apart, leaving only broken hearts and shattered dreams.

I slowly moved from the bed, trying my hardest not to wake him. I was a coward and I wasn't afraid to admit it. I just didn't want to see Logan's face if he had to watch me leave. It would kill me. I loved him enough not to put him through anymore shit from my past, a past that rips through my present and taints my future.

Sliding out from the bed, I frantically looked for all my clothes, finding my phone on the floor by my panties. It was on silent, but the screen was screaming at me that I had missed several calls. Picking up my phone, I swiped my finger across the screen to reveal the total destruction I had caused. Angel's name appeared before I could see the damage, shit. I had left the party last night without telling anyone where I was going, including Angel. I'll call him later, right now I needed to get back to my dorm.

Quickly picking up my clothes, I ran into Logan's bathroom, throwing my clothes down on the floor before stepping towards the sink. Looking into the mirror, I gasped from the reflection that stared back at me. My eyes sparkled without the use of makeup, my cheeks were glowing a perfect pink and my hair looked glossy. My body glowed while my mind splintered in two. I was such a horrible bitch. Tears stung my eyes as I hurriedly threw my clothes on, knowing I wasn't just about to do the walk of shame, I was doing the walk of 'the bitch who just broke her best friend's heart'.

Taking a deep breath, I walked out of the bathroom to find the bed empty. Where was Logan? Shit, I didn't want to do this face-to-face. I wanted to sneak out and be the cowardly bitch that I was. But before I could leave, I heard the door swing open. Turning around, I saw Logan taking heaving breaths looking at me with wide eyes.

Tears stung my eyes as I watched Logan run his hands over

his handsome face as he gasped for breath, had he gone for a run? I bit my lip hard as I watched a single bead of sweat run down the side of his face, a face that was only last night snuggled close into my neck.

"Where did you go?" Logan asked as he walked into the room, kicking the door shut behind him.

"I was getting dressed." I replied as heat flamed my face, the reason why I was naked this morning staring me right in the face.

"I thought...I thought you left." He uttered so quietly that I almost didn't hear him.

"I was." I whispered as I moved my gaze to my feet, not wanting to look him in the eyes anymore.

"You were going to walk out of here while I was still asleep?" My eyes quickly snapped towards his as his voice raised with his question. "After everything, you were going to just fucking leave?"

"Yes." The tears fell quickly and freely as I watched pain flash across Logan's face. His brows furrowed as he tried to take in what I had just said.

"I'm sorry."

It was pathetic. I was pathetic. Sorry wasn't going to fix anything nor was it going to help, but all I could do was watch as Logan's eyes turned into something I had never seen before. He was angry, angry at me.

"Save your fucking apologies, Neva." He said before angrily wiping away tears that had escaped his eyes. "We both understood that this was only one night, but I hoped that maybe when I finally told you how I fucking feel, that maybe you wouldn't rip my heart out."

I gasped as I watched more tears drop onto his cheeks, his

eyes now bloodshot and his face tear stained.

"You have ripped my fucking heart out, Neva and what's worse is that I love you far too fucking much to hate you for it."

I couldn't hold back the sobs that threatened to escape as the tears spilled from my eyes. It was then that I realized that in trying to protect my own heart, I had shattered another.

"I'm sorry, I'm so sorry."

The words tasted sour as they poured from my mouth, as the enormity of what I had done hit me, hard. Throwing my hand over my mouth as I tried to stop the sobs from escaping further, what had I done?

"Logan, I -" I started as I took a step forward but Logan swiftly cut me off with a shake of his head.

"I'll keep my promise, I'll leave you alone." He said closing his eyes as he quickly sucked in a breath.

"Logan." I didn't know what to say. What do I say to the man I loved…The man who laid his heart out to me…The man who had made love to me?

"Please." He pleaded as a sob broke from his lips. "Just go." He stepped further away from the door, indicating for me to leave.

I didn't know what I was more afraid of, Logan breaking my heart or me shattering his. I needed to tell him, I needed him to understand why. Taking a deep shaky breath, I made my way towards the door, there was no use trying to apologize to him. It was clear 'sorry' wasn't going to make a difference, I had hurt him. Deeply.

As I reached the door, I quickly turned to face him, his eyes wide, not knowing what I was doing. But, I had to do this. I had to make him understand. Before Logan could react, I placed my palm against his cheek, which was now soaked in tears, killing me further.

"You scare the shit out of me, Logan." I said, watching as Logan's face flashed with shock. "You know me on a level that no one else does, you see the real me, the broken me."

I closed my eyes, remembering the night of one of my worst nightmares I had ever had to endure. I was fifteen, and Logan had been pulling me out of my hellish nightmares for four years, always by my side when I need him most...until that night.

Tate and Logan had been invited to a house party, Logan was reluctant to go, worried that I would need him when he wasn't around. I was quickly becoming sick of my nightmares tying him down, tying him to me. But I soon regretted that decision when I was once again pulled into the shadows. Darkness seeped through every fiber of my being as I was restrained under another spine-chilling torment.

I was being tortured. The demons were killing me emotionally, breaking me physically, thrown right back to the day at the hospital. I was pinned to the ceiling above my father's body, desperately watching as a scared ten-year-old me was being ripped apart from her father. My wrists were pinned, outstretched beside me, the grip becoming tighter and tighter as the minutes passed. Pain shot through my body as I watched a doctor walk into the room, unable to scream as another hand wrapped around my throat.

Tears spilled from my cheeks as I watched a doctor turn off the machines that were keeping my father alive, the lines on the screens flattening out as my father silently slipped away. I wanted so much to comfort him, struggling against my captors, but they were unrelenting. They pinned me down tighter against the ceiling, torturing me further.

A cloud of black smoke suddenly covered my body, only to disappear seconds later. My eyes struggled to adjust to the different lighting. My eyes widened as I looked around, the scent of car fumes penetrating my nostrils...I was on the bridge again, a demon floating over my body once more.

In a wave of panic my mom had called Tate and Logan, unable to wake me from my nightmare as my demons carried on the painful onslaught. They broke me into tiny little fragments, controlling me, and tearing every last shred of my spirit.

*"I will always love you.*

*I will always protect you.*

*I will always keep you safe."*

Three tiny promises penetrated through the darkness as searing pain ran through me, my throat feeling as though someone had slashed it with a razor. I was crying out, screaming in pain for both my ten-year-old self and the father I would never be able to get back. My demons were locked away until the next night of painful memories would wash over me, guarded by my protector as he soothed my shivering skin. My erratic heartbeat settled as the sobs calmed into silent hiccups. He had come to protect me, to save me from my demons once again, pushing them back into the abyss.

Tears spilled down my face as I stopped the memory taking me further into my past, realizing that he had spoken the same words when he was making love to me. I gently stroked away a single tear from Logan's cheek as I tried to explain further.

"You have seen me in my darkest moments, those earth-shattering, gut wrenching moments where I am pulled right back to that day in the hospital. You have seen my pain and suffering and that is why we can't do this, Logan. My grief could tear us apart."

My tears were constant and unrelenting as I took a shaky breath and continued.

"My past will tear us apart, don't you see that? With Angel I can pretend I am normal, not the broken Neva that you know or see. The look in Angel's eyes isn't sorrow or pity, it is fire, want and need. He doesn't know me."

Logan's eyes closed as he sucked in a breath once more.

"I need you, Neva." He croaked before biting his bottom lip.

"I know, but it's time I protected you. I need to protect you, I need to keep you safe, from me."

The more I spoke, the more I lost a piece of myself to Logan, his face was a picture of heartbreak. I had done that, and I fucking hate myself for it. I slowly wiped away one more of Logan's tears with the pad of my thumb, smiling weakly at him.

"I'm sorry." I whispered, before leaning in and briefly grazing my lips against Logan's cheek.

I didn't wait for a reply as I quickly opened the door and left Logan behind, making my way down the corridor before suddenly stopping in my tracks, hearing Logan's breaking voice.

"Stay safe, Neva."

"Always." I said, knowing he wouldn't have heard me as I walked out of the building. Leaving behind the man I loved with a broken heart.

# nineteen

"**W**HERE THE HELL HAVE YOU BEEN?" Low snapped as I made my way into our dorm.

"Not now, Low." I shot, hiding my tear-stained face with my hair as I made a bee line for the bathroom. I slammed the door shut and locked it tight behind me.

"What's going on, Neva?" Low asked from behind the door, her voice taking a calmer tone than before.

Placing the palms of my hands against the wall in front of me I let my head bow, the tears now coming thick and fast as I was no longer able to hold in the gut-clenching sobs that escaped.

"Shit." I cried before throwing the palm of my hand against the wall.

I let the sobs take over my body, allowing them to consume me. The tears melted together on my cheeks as my lips burned from the saltiness of my pain. I was doing this to protect him, to protect me. Frustration took over as I silently cursed the man that caused all the pain, all the suffering. The man that broke me into millions of pieces and left me to put them back together; the bastard that killed my father.

Justice was served, they said. My ass, justice was served! The man who killed my father was injured in the accident. They were just cuts and scrapes compared to what my dad went through. Once he was released as a patient he was arrested, charged with Vehicular Manslaughter. We were told he pleaded guilty and was sentenced to ten years. Thankfully, we didn't have to go through further trauma of going to court. Ten years wasn't enough, it was never enough.

"Shit." I slammed my palm against the wall again, for the pain he had caused and the pain I had caused. How was I any better than him?

"Shit. Shit. Shit. Shit." Ugly, angry sobs racked my body as I slammed both of my hands against the wall one last time. As my knees buckled from underneath me, my body slowly slid down the wall, dragging my stinging palms with it.

Emotions I haven't felt in years overcame me as I lay in a heap on the floor. Low's voice was trying to cut through my loud, hard sobs.

Hate.

Guilt.

Heartbreak.

Nausea.

Nausea.

Shit.

Throwing my ringing hand over my mouth, I scrambled to the toilet, just in time to throw up the contents of my stomach. I wondered if I could throw up my heart? Maybe then I could see if it truly was broken, cracked, and unfixable.

Bile burned my throat like liquid lava as I heaved into the bowl once more, letting the pain pour from my mouth violently. My heaving drowned out Low, who was now frantically banging on the bathroom door, threatening to kick the door in.

After finally being able to breathe without throwing up again, I placed my forehead against the cool toilet seat, using it to prop up my weak body, not sure if I was going to throw up again.

Somewhere between my forehead meeting the toilet seat and my breathing coming back to normal, I suddenly screamed. The sound of splintering wood and a large cracking sound made my stomach turn once more, turning my head to what was left of the bathroom door I found Tate staring at me wide-eyed.

"What's wrong, baby girl?" Tate asked, his voice laced with concern as he made his way over to me. He stepped over pieces of wood that had been thrown across the bathroom from the sheer force of his foot.

I was still trying to process why the freaking bathroom door was now splintered into tiny pieces all over my bathroom floor. But Tate's strong arms wrapped around my shoulders, throwing my thoughts of the door out of my mind as my body melted into my brothers.

Tate slowly sat on the floor, pulling me onto his lap as I placed my head on his chest. His arms acted like a cocoon as if he was shielding me, this was home. There was no talking, only the sound of my sobs as Tate rocked me slowly. It reminded me of the day I was rocking my mom that same way.

I didn't know if it was minutes or hours that had passed

when I felt Tate's body tense, lifting my head I looked at him wondering what was wrong.

"My ass has gone numb." He whispered, breaking an unexpected chuckle from my lips.

"Your shirt." I said as I noticed tear stains in his crisp white shirt.

"It's okay, I have others." He replied, laying his cheek on top of my head as he stroked my hair away from my face.

Nodding, I melted back into my brother, noticing he still hadn't moved even though he complained about his ass going numb. Tate's chest rose and fell quickly against my cheek before he sighed.

"You're not going to tell me, are you?" He asked, clearly saddened that whatever I was going through I couldn't tell him.

"No." I stated, as I slowly moved my weight from my brother's lap and stood up on shaky legs. "But you don't have to worry about me. I can take care of myself."

"I know that, Neva, but you know you can talk to me about anything, right?" He asked, but I had to look away from him. What he just said wasn't exactly true. I couldn't tell him about Logan nor could I talk to him about dad.

Ever since dad died, Tate had just seemed to block it out. I don't remember him ever crying. I just remember a child who grew up very quickly in a short space of time. Tate was my rock, but I could see he was close to crumbling. It seemed I was grieving for both of us.

"I know." I nodded, trying not to break and tell my brother everything.

"Whatever it is, Neva, it will be okay." He said as he got back on his feet, wincing as he rubbed his ass, trying to get some blood flow back.

I could only smile at him, if only he knew.

*twenty*

After an hour of reassuring Tate and Low that I was fine, they reluctantly left the dorm. I hadn't told them about Logan but I had a feeling Low knew, her 'we will talk later' face told me all I needed to know.

Finally on my own, I fell on to my bed with a hard thud as I ran over the past 24 hours in my head. Logan's hands, lips and body against mine; the way he touched me delicately, as if I was fragile and breakable. But the images of Logan's naked body against mine was soon washed away when the memory of his face this morning took over. He had pleaded with me and declared his love for me and I couldn't find the strength to tell him that I loved him too. But what was worse was that even when I was curled up in Logan's arms, I didn't once think about Angel.

Angel...Fuck.

What the hell was wrong with me? I had a perfect boyfriend who was hot, sexy and sinful, but also funny and intelligent. The more I thought about how perfect Angel was, the more apparent it became that I was so imperfect, so fucked up. There was no way I could tell him about what had happened between Logan and me. I just couldn't do that to him, I won't do that to him.

I had already shattered two hearts, I wasn't going to shatter a third.

Suddenly my phone started ringing, leaning over my bed to the bedside cabinet I picked it up before staring at the screen.

Angel...

Shit, I knew I had to talk to him but did it have to be right now? Angel definitely thought so as my phone would not stop ringing. Tentatively I ran my finger across the screen before putting it to my ear.

"Angel." I rasped, my voice trembling.

"Shit, Neva, where are you? Are you okay? I have been calling you all night! I have been worried sick."

"I'm sorry." I said quickly. "I felt sick and went to my brothers, I crashed there last night." I cringed at my lie.

"You're sick?" Angel asked, clearly still concerned.

"Yeah, I'm fine now. It must have just been a bug." The lie was pouring out of my mouth, and it just wouldn't stop.

"Do you want me to come over?" Angel asked.

"No it's okay, I'm going over to see my mom today so I might just crash there until class on Monday."

"Are you sure?"

"Yeah, it will give me some time to get the assignment done for class too." God I was such a bitch.

"Okay baby, I'll see you Monday. Call me if you need anything."

"Yeah, see you Monday."

I chewed my lip hard as the call disconnected. I had just lied through my damn teeth to my boyfriend because I didn't have the backbone to tell him about where I actually was. Tears quickly formed in my eyes as I swallowed the distinct taste of copper. Releasing my lip, I wiped at the corner of my mouth with the back of my hand to find a streak of blood against my skin. It was time to do what I knew best.

Run.

Pulling out my suitcase from the closet, I threw it onto my bed, tossing enough clothes inside for the weekend. I was going to take my own advice and stay at mom's for the weekend. I needed some time to understand everything and make some decisions about what the hell I was going to do.

Turning to my bedside cabinet I opened the drawer, finding my black leather notepad and pencil I quickly ripped out a page and wrote a note out to Low.

*Gone to mom's for the weekend, be home soon. Neva x*

A single tear dropped on to the note before me, the words I had haphazardly written taking me right back to ten years before.

Dad had asked me if I wanted to go with him for a trip to the store. He had dangled his keys to the truck in front of me. His secret sign that only I would understand. He was going to show me how to drive again. A devilish twinkle appeared in his eyes as it always did when we did something mom didn't approve of. Mom didn't know dad had been teaching me how to drive for the last six months. We knew she wouldn't be happy, but we still did it anyway, it was our little secret.

It was one of my favorite memories of my dad. He would

take me to an old parking lot just a couple of miles outside of Spring Water and put the truck in park while I climbed onto his lap. I wasn't tall enough to work the pedals but I could steer. Dad would work the gas while he guided my hands through the steering wheel.

But that night, I decided to stay home. Frost had started to creep onto the edges of the windows in the house as Christmas approached closer with each passing day. I slowly shook my head at my dad smiling before turning my attention back to the TV, my dad chuckled before sighing.

"I'll just have to get a cold butt on my own then."

"Daddy, you won't get a cold butt. It's warm in the truck." I giggled as I turned back to my dad.

"What if I sit on the ice cream?" He asked in mock horror. "My butt might just freeze and fall off!"

"Daddy, that sounds like a good idea. Your butt stinks!" I said laughing hard at my own joke.

"Young lady! Have you smelled yours? You most certainly take after my side of the family." He winked before taking the few strides into the room, pulling me into his arms and kissing me on the head. "We will prove that to your mother later. Now go and get your homework finished so we can eat some ice cream when I get back."

I simply nodded and turned my attention back to the TV once more, hearing my dad chuckle and walk out the room making his way to the front door.

"Be home soon." He shouted over his shoulder, which in turn had us all replying a swift 'okay' in unison.

Tears streamed down my face as I recalled that last

conversation with my dad before the accident. Why did they take my dad? Why didn't they take the scum bag who had killed him instead?

Shaking my head, I placed the note on Low's pillow before throwing my phone on my bed. If I was going to stay at my mom's I needed complete peace and no doubt I will be inundated with texts and phone calls from Low checking up on me. I loved that girl like a sister, but sometimes she could be a little overbearing.

Once I was finally happy that I had packed everything I had needed for my weekend at moms, I walked back over to the closet to pick up my guitar. I wasn't sure how mom would feel with me bringing it to the house, but I decided I needed to take a piece of my dad with me.

Quickly slinging the guitar over my shoulder by the strap, I picked up my suitcase from the bed, turning around in a full circle. When I was sure I had everything I needed, I took a deep breath. I walked out of the dorm and right off campus.

After making sure no one had spotted me, I started walking in the direction of my mom's house, my luggage secured in my right hand while my guitar hung over my shoulder. I placed my headphones into my ears, an old Motown record that my father loved to listen to played through the speakers. I stared out into the sunset, taking in the crisp, cool air, wondering what the hell to do.

*twenty-one*

"**Y**OUR DAD USED TO DRIVE ME nuts with that thing." My mom's voice pulled me out from my day dream as I stared at the house.

"I remember, you threatened to cut all of the strings." I smiled to myself at the memory.

*Mom had been finishing off some work for her job as a project manager at the time and dad was trying to teach me how to play the guitar, I was never any good. Where my dad's fingers would lightly stroke the strings and produce a beautiful sound, mine would strum hard, creating a screeching noise that would put a drowning cat to shame.*

*I remember her stomping into the living room with her paperwork in one hand and her reading glasses in the other, her shoulders showing signs of stress and her nose wrinkling from the horrible noise I was producing.*

*"Brandon, dear." She said sweetly. "For the love of all things holy*

will you please go and play that thing somewhere else so I can get some work done?"

Dad chuckled at mom's little outburst. She was a bit stressed lately after she was promoted to project manager at work. She was working for an interior design firm and loved it. Our house was all the evidence you needed to know her love for interior design.

"Come on, Neva, let's give your mom some peace and quiet." Dad said as he led us outside to the porch swing. Sitting down, he started to strum a tune I hadn't heard him play before. It was soft and sweet mixed with a gritty edge and I loved it.

I embedded the sound of the song in my head. Even though I didn't know how to play the guitar, I was adamant that one day I would learn that piece of music.

"Brandon!! I will cut the strings off that thing if you don't go away!" Mom shouted from her office window.

"Yeah, I did. Didn't I?" Mom laughed softly, pulling me back from the memory.

"Is it okay that I brought it with me?" I asked, I didn't want to cause mom any more pain that she had already endured. She had been through enough.

"Of course I don't mind sweetheart, but it wasn't the guitar that concerned me." She said as she raised an eyebrow at me.

"Can't a daughter see her mother at the weekend?" I asked in mock horror.

"Sarcasm is so unbecoming of you, Neva." She replied with a soft chuckle.

With that, I picked up my suitcase from the sidewalk and followed my mom into the house. Shutting the door behind me, the scent of cranberries hit me as I made my way down the hall. Mom was always lighting candles during the day, she said it helped with her designing.

Looking around the hallway, I smiled as I noticed all the family pictures hanging inside beautiful frames. Most of them were of Tate and me when we were kids but after every two photos of us there would be a photo of us all with dad. Somewhere we had been on our fishing vacation, mom had groaned at the idea while dad, Tate and I smiled.

Walking further down the hallway, I placed my suitcase and guitar at the bottom of the staircase before making my way into the kitchen where mom was making coffee.

"You look just like him, Neva." Mom said while stirring her coffee.

"I don't know if that is a good thing." I replied as I took a seat at the dining table.

"What? Why?" She asked as she placed my coffee in front of me before taking a seat opposite, holding her cup in her hands.

I shrugged, I wanted so much to apologize for looking so much like the man she lost. I can't imagine how she felt looking at me every day and seeing her dead husband.

"I am so grateful for it, Neva. I am grateful that a part of your father lives in you. I am grateful that you act so much like him without even knowing it and I am grateful that you didn't go with him that night." I watched as mom's eyes glossed over with unshed tears, her face a picture of pain.

"Me too." I said as I placed my hand in hers, squeezing it gently.

"So, are you going to tell me what brought you here?" She asked, changing the subject and eying me suspiciously.

"I just wanted to see you, mom." I lied. It seemed I was doing a lot of that lately.

"Okay." She replied, shaking her head slightly.

"What? You're not going to even try and get it out of me?" I asked, shocked. Usually she would pry and pry until I broke and told her.

"No, you'll tell me when you're ready." She said as the edge of her lip formed into a small smile.

"Who are you and what did you do with my mom?" I joked. This was so out of character for her. What was going on?

I watched as she threw her head back and released a hearty laugh; a laugh so pure that it took me a couple of minutes to remember the last time I had heard her laugh. It was before the accident.

"I'm still here, sweetheart, trust me, so don't be getting any ideas of getting drunk and pregnant just because I'm not pushing you for information about your social life." She chuckled.

"Yes, ma'am." I saluted before dipping my hand into the cookie jar on the table.

After giving my mom a kiss good night I made my way up the staircase to my old bedroom. The house had three bedrooms, each having their own en-suite. Opening my door, I stepped inside finding it just as I had left it. The far wall in front of me was a deep scarlet while the other three were an off-white. My large, king sized bed sat against the scarlet wall. The metal frame was a brilliant black with matching black silk sheets. The bedroom furniture was a perfect dark tone of black, while my carpet was an off-white, matching the three other walls.

I had missed my room. Mom had decorated it for my

birthday three years ago and I couldn't have been happier with it. Making my way over to the bed, I placed my suitcase and guitar at my feet before running the palm of my hand against the silky soft sheets on the bed and smiling. Turning to face the wall behind me, tears filled my eyes as I stared at the photo of dad and me. He was cradling me in his arms. I was just hours old, but there was no doubt even then that I was a daddy's girl. As my tiny hand wrapped around his index finger, you could see the love in my father's eyes as he looked into the camera smiling.

Sighing, I turned to my guitar. Picking it up, I sat on my bed and cradled it in my lap. I remembered something my dad had once said about the perfect way to hold a guitar.

"You need to cradle it gently like a newborn baby, but strum it like you would a woman." I laughed as I remembered my reaction.

"Ew, daddy!" I said as I crunched up my nose.

Taking my dad's advice, I slowly started to strum the chords, wondering what to play; but before I could decide, my fingers did it for me. The unmistakable tune that my dad had once played to me on the porch swing all those years ago graced my ears. The tune brought back beautiful memories of my dad. How determined he was to teach me to play and how he taught me never to give up when I failed.

I quickly became frustrated like I did every time I played the chords that were forever embedded in my mind. I could never finish it nor could I put a name to it. Dad had never finished the song that day on the porch and I regretted every day that I never asked him to play it for me again. I regretted a lot of things when it came to my father.

Sighing in defeat, I placed my guitar by my bed before opening my case to change into some pajamas. I came across an envelope. It was folded down the middle and when I opened it up, I noticed it was addressed to me. It was the letter that I had stuffed into my pocket when I was here last. Curious as to who would send me a letter, I quickly sat on the bed and tore it open. As I pulled out the letter, I felt something drop into my lap. Fumbling on the bed, I searched for the mysterious object, wondering what the hell it was. Finally I managed to grasp it between my fingertips, bringing it up to eye level to inspect it.

I gasped. It was a guitar pick, my dad's guitar pick. It was an electric blue with inscriptions on both sides in cursive script. On one side, it read Brandon and when I flipped it over, it read James. Gripping it in my palm I turned to the letter, why had I been sent dad's guitar pick? I slowly opened the letter. My hands were shaking and my breathing loud as I started to read it.

> *My sweet baby girl,*
> *If this letter has reached you then I am so sorry, I could only hope that it doesn't come to much of a shock.*
> *First I want to explain. I know that you're wondering what is going on, so I will try my best to tell you what this is all about.*
> *Do you remember Mrs. Scott? She was the sweet lady down the street that used to have the biggest apple tree we had ever seen. We used to ask her for some of those delicious apples so we could eat them when we had picnics. Well, she had a son named Khai, he was such a fearless little boy, a boy any father would be proud of. But one summer, he was too fearless. He had climbed the same apple tree in their backyard and fell. He died right there in his mother's arms. It broke her heart into millions of pieces and all we could do was watch as she grieved.*

*After watching Mrs. Scott grieve so hard for the loss of her son, I started writing this letter. I decided after I had written it that I would send it to my solicitor should anything happen to me. Should this letter find its way to you then it means you are nearing the beautiful age of twenty-one and I am not with you to celebrate, I'm sorry.*

*In life, tragedy and loss happens every single day and nobody is immune. There are only two certainties in this world. You are born into this life and you will also be taken from it too. Some will be taken without warning and some will be taken slowly. It is the cruelest of certainties and also the most powerful. You will grieve for the loss but you will also become a stronger person for the gift of love and memories that you received.*

*I didn't want to leave this life without giving you that gift, the gift of love and memories. My guitar pick is the gift of memories. It is our memories of playing my guitar. This letter is the gift of love. It is my love for you my sweet baby girl.*

*Neva, I love you unconditionally and I always will. You are sweet, kindhearted, and an absolute breath of fresh air. Don't let anyone tell you different. Life is hard and complicated and sometimes we want to give up, but just remember, you are loved and cherished. Don't let life slip you by, take hold of it and never let go.*

*Life isn't about waiting for the storm to pass, it's learning to dance in the rain.*

*Dance in the rain, Neva.*
*Love, Daddy.*

My tears were a constant stream of emotions as I re-read my father's words over and over again. I must have read that letter another twenty times before I felt another sheet of paper sitting behind it. Placing the letter carefully on the bed, a sob broke from my mouth when I took in what was in my hands.

It was a music sheet, with chords and lyrics. It was the song

I could never finish or name. But now, it had a name and lyrics, but most of all, it had an ending.

I scanned the lyrics until my eyes found the chorus, my heart breaking as the words sunk in.

*I will find you in the rain,*
*I will break through any storm*
*Just to be with you always, to keep you safe and warm.*
*In my arms may you stay,*
*So close to my heart*
*Holding on forever until the day we are ripped apart.*
*I am yours forever, don't you see?*
*That I'm a stronger man for finding you,*
*For finding me.*

He had titled it 'Finding You.'

I gently folded the letters back into the envelope. Placing it in one hand and holding the pick with the other, I silently I cried myself to sleep, clutching onto three of life's most important things.

The gift of love, the gift of memories and the gift of music.

*twenty-two*

THE NEXT MORNING I FOUND myself at the mercy of my guitar, softly strumming the beautiful tune with my father's pick trying to play the song that was once an enigma for so long. I played slowly, as if trying to make the chords seep into my skin. I tried to absorb it, like a sponge soaking up every last drop of liquid.

The more I played, the more I stared at the picture of my father and me on the opposite wall. But this time, I didn't cry nor did I want too. Instead, I smiled, knowing that while I played, I remembered. I held onto those sweet memories of a man who truly was a hero.

Sometime later, I finally pried my aching hands from the guitar and walked down the staircase, my step faltering as I stood outside the kitchen door. It wasn't the voice of my mother and a stranger talking that stopped me mid stride, it was the hearty laugh that erupted from my mother's mouth. It seemed something or someone had finally managed to bring back something neither Tate or I could, laughter.

"It will be fine Lorena, I promise." I overhead the stranger's voice saying as I leaned my head closer to the door, it was a man's voice.

"I know, I just don't want to upset her, Marcus. I had it all planned out to tell her and this was not how I imagined it going." Mom replied.

Who was Marcus? I decided to stop eavesdropping on my mom and make my way into the kitchen. But when I opened the door I was not prepared for the sight that greeted me, really not prepared. Mom's chest pressed against a man's body while her hands ran through his hair, his hands resting on her waist. Mom was sucking face, I may need to bleach my eyes after this. As if that wasn't embarrassing enough, the moan that escaped my mom's lips certainly was. Yeah, I will definitely need to bleach my eyes.

Not wanting to witness anymore, I coughed hard before walking into the kitchen. Taking my usual seat at the table, I placed my elbows on the table and interlocked my fingers together before resting my chin on top. I watched as they jumped apart, like teenagers caught making out by their parents; funny how roles switch in the blink of an eye.

From the corner of my eye, I took in the stranger who was looking just as shocked as my mother was, but it wasn't his expression that took me by surprise. It was his handsome good looks, short blond hair matched with a chiseled jaw. Deep gray eyes and his skin a perfect sun kissed glow, he was probably in his mid-forties but could easily pass off being in his mid-thirties.

"Good morning." Mom whispered, clearly horrified as she tried to hide the blush that was currently spreading across her cheeks.

"Good morning, momma." I said with a smile on my face before turning to Marcus with an eyebrow raised. "Good morning, Marcus."

The look of pure shock registered on Marcus's face at the realization I had used his name, clearly understanding I had overheard them talking.

"Oh, God." Mom groaned as she buried her face in her hands. "I'm so sorry, Neva." Her apology slightly muffled against her palms.

"Why are you sorry?" I asked, confused as to why she was apologizing to me.

"You weren't meant to find out like this, I was going to tell you after your birthday." She replied, slowly pulling her face from her hands before she took the seat opposite me at the table.

I could only watch as tears spilled down her beautiful face. I hated seeing mom cry. She was so strong after everything she had been through that sometimes I forget that for us to feel strong, we have to experience feeling weak.

"I'm so happy for you." I smiled, and I was. Mom deserved to be happy and if her happiness meant being with Marcus, then that was all that mattered.

I knew that mom would always love my dad, they were inseparable. They were childhood sweethearts, and when they decided to both go to college, mom had followed dad half way across the country so they could be together. I remember the small things, dad holding mom's hand when they didn't think we were looking. The way they could find each other across a crowded room so easily or even the stolen kisses. Their love was never-ending and eternal. I could only hope I could experience even a tiny shred of what they had.

Unrelenting, unyielding, unfaltering love.

But after dad was cruelly ripped away from her, part of her died with him. I just hoped that maybe someday she would get it back.

"Thank you, sweetheart." Mom's voice quickly cut through my thoughts.

"I'm going to give you two some space Lor, I'll call you later." Marcus said before placing a tender kiss on my mom's cheek. Smiling, we both watched as he left through the front door.

"Wow." I said as I smiled back at mom. "Well, I certainly wasn't expecting to see that when I woke up this morning." I joked as I watched mom blush furiously for the second time.

"I'm so sorry you had to see that, are you sure you're okay with this?" She asked tentatively.

"Mom, if he makes you happy, then I'm more than okay with it." I answered her question truthfully.

"You know no one will ever replace your father, he holds a special place in my heart and he always will." She said before pausing, as if choosing her words carefully. "But I love Marcus dearly, it is no bigger of a love nor is it any less. It is a different kind of love, a new kind of love but a familiar one too." She finished, releasing a shaky breath that I didn't realize she was holding.

"I know, and I am so glad to hear you laugh again mom." I said as tears filled my eyes. "Now spill, how did you meet him?"

For the next hour mom told me all about Marcus and the day they met, all with a bright smile on her face. They had met six months ago. Mom was in her studio looking over her new fabric swatches that had arrived that very morning. She was so engrossed in her work that she didn't even notice the man leaning over her shoulder to see what had captured her attention so intently. Well, that was until his breath had grazed her neck, she jumped quick and fast. She was startled by the stranger over her shoulder that her arms threw out in shock, causing her right hand to connect with his nose. Blood had poured everywhere; on his shirt, the fabric swatches and even her desk. Once she realized what she had done, she apologized profusely while attending to the poor man's nose. She even offered to pay the dry cleaning bill for his shirt.

"It was an accident, don't worry." He had said to her while pinching the bridge of his nose, trying to stop the blood from dripping anywhere else.

"Please, I insist. Let me get it dry cleaned for you. It's the least I could do." She pleaded, glad that it was only his shirt that had the most damage. Thankfully she hadn't hit him hard enough to break his nose.

"Really, it's fine. Don't worry about it. I'm Marcus Young, by the way." He said, placing his hand in hers while still pinching his nose with the other.

"Lorena James, it's nice to meet you. Will you please at least let me take it? It's only a couple of blocks down the road." The words were barely out of her mouth when Marcus had swiftly pulled the shirt from his back and placed it in her hands, gasping she tried to avert her eyes but she couldn't stop looking at his sculptured body.

The shirt never made it to the dry cleaners that day.

"He just took his shirt off right there in your studio?" I asked wide eyed.

"Oh, yeah." Mom replied with a wicked grin on her face.

"Mom, mind out of gutter please. So what happened next?"

She only raised an eyebrow at my question while a tint of blush covered her cheeks.

"Conversation over." I said quickly, causing us to both laugh so hard tears had streamed down our cheeks.

The rest of the weekend flew by quickly, mom had decided to make it a girly weekend with manicures and pedicures, retail therapy and a movie night with face masks and popcorn. I think she was trying to make it up to me for not telling me about Marcus sooner. She really felt bad for keeping it to herself.

Sunday night was here before I knew it. I was in my bedroom packing away my clothes into my bag when mom knocked on my door.

"Hey, momma." I said over my shoulder while folding a pair of jeans.

"Are you nearly ready?" She asked.

"Yeah, just packing the last few things."

"Okay, oh did you open that letter you got?" I froze, what do I tell her?

"Erm, yeah."

"It was from your father, wasn't it?"

"Mom..." I said as I turned around, expecting her to be upset but instead she was, smiling.

"It's okay Neva, Tate got one when he was twenty-one too. I

just hope it will help you with trying to work through whatever brought you here." She said before making her way over to me, pulling me into a hug. "Just promise me that whatever you do, you do it for you." She whispered into my hair before pulling away and walking out of my room.

# twenty-three

WALKING ONTO CAMPUS LATER that night, I had no idea what to expect. What happens if Logan decided to tell Angel? What if Angel finds out? Shaking my head, I made my way to my dorm room, I needed to stop thinking about it. It is my own fault no matter what happens. I fucked over the man I love for the man who doesn't know me and all because I want to pretend. I want to pretend that I was normal and not broken. I would do anything to stop the looks of pity. That included breaking my own heart.

Opening the door to my dorm, I was suddenly lifted from my feet, dropping my bag in the process.

"Oh my God! I have missed you!" Low squealed as she finally stopped suffocating me within her arms.

"Okay, Low you can put me down now." I said laughing.

Low released me from her grasp, finally having my feet planted on the floor, I straightened my blouse and smiled at my best friend.

"Miss me that much, huh?" I asked, laughing.

"Of course I missed you, woman! Now, sit the hell down." Low's voice quickly changed and her smile faded. Oh shit.

Picking up my case that was still on the floor in the doorway I placed it at the foot of my bed while Low shut the door, this was not good. I just hope she doesn't ask why I left in such a hurry and without my phone. I don't think I could tell her even if she asked.

Sitting on the edge of my bed, I watched as Low walked towards her bed. She sat down and gave me a pointed stare.

"Are you up for a game?" She asked, cocking her brow, I didn't like the sound of that.

"Sure." I said sheepishly.

"Okay, so the game is called 'Screwing'." She said. "I am going to ask you some questions and you are going to answer them, but instead of saying 'yes' you will say 'screw you' and instead of 'no' you answer 'screw him'. Get it?"

"Yeah, I think so."

"Okay, first question. Did you run to your momma's because of two certain men, whose names I won't mention?" She asked.

"Well, fuck me Low." I sighed. "Straight for the jugular!"

"Answer the damn question, Neva, you owe me that much." I flinched at the sound her voice.

"Screw you." I smirked.

"Nicely done." She said with a small smile. "That night when you found out what Logan had done to Tate's eye, did you see Logan?"

"Screw you." I sighed.

"You didn't come home that night. Did you stay in Logan and Tate's room?"

"Screw you."

"Does Angel know you stayed the night there?"

"Screw him."

"Oh, I wouldn't mind baby doll." She replied quickly, winking at me. "Okay, did you sleep in your brother's bed?"

I drew in a quick breath. Low knew that Logan comforted me in the past and we had shared a bed innocently a few times. She would know just from my answer what had happened, especially knowing that Logan and I had kissed not that long ago. And if I lied, she would know. She always knows.

"Screw him."

"Oh my God Neva! Did you sleep with Logan?"

Oh. Shit!

"No! I mean screw him, I mean no. No!" Quickly throwing my hand over my mouth I fought back the tears that were threatening to escape.

"Oh. My. God." Low gasped, mirroring me as she placed her hand over her mouth in utter shock. "You slept with Logan, Neva what on earth were you thinking?"

"Oh God, Low, what am I going to do?" I asked as tears poured down my face and the guilt seeped through to my veins once more, my body feeling the full force of my decisions.

"Oh. My. God." Low repeated once more. "How could you? You...Logan...What the fuck? Jesus Neva, I don't know what to say." I watched as she started pacing the room.

I couldn't blame her. Shit, I don't even know what to say either. What I did was unforgivable, I won't deny it. I did the worst thing you can do to a person. I took his trust, broke it, ripped it apart and then handed it back, while still hoping he could still trust me like before. I had done that, I wasn't proud of it but the feelings I have for Logan are so strong and intense that I couldn't deny it either.

"Low..."

"Why Neva? Why? You have a boyfriend who worships the fucking ground you walk on and yet you sleep with the man whore?" She spat, her voice becoming strained.

"You don't understand, Low! Nobody understands. When I am with Angel I can forget who I am, forget my past, I can just live and be normal. He doesn't know about the nightmares or what fuels them, he just wants me. But then there is Logan, who has become more than the young boy who used to watch over me after the nightmares that drained every shred of fight from my body. He has become the man who I have fallen for... hard. He is the only person who understands who I am, but that comes at a price. My past and everything that is in it will tear us apart. I can't go a damn day without images of that night in the hospital clouding my vision, even clouding my judgment." Taking a deep breath I continued. "With Angel I can just pretend, I'm no longer broken or tainted. I am just Neva James. What happened between Logan and I was something I wanted to happen, but in doing that I have broken his fucking heart, and shattered mine too. But we could never work." Tears were coming thick and fast as I watched Low's reaction to what I had just revealed.

"Okay."

Okay? What did she mean okay? There was no bitching, no fighting. Nothing.

"Huh?" I asked.

"I may not fucking like it or understand it, but this is your decision, Neva. Just let me know when you need me to pick up the pieces. Because this is going to be one big God damned mess!" She said before picking up her jacket and leaving the room.

As I sat on my bed, my thoughts drifted back to Angel, and how much I would hurt him if I told him exactly what I had done. I am sick of hurting and sick of hurting people, it was in that moment that I decided I wasn't going to tell him. I was going to get on with my life and as much as it pained me to admit, I needed to forget Logan. I needed to forget what we had shared that night and all the nights that he held me after my horrible nightmares, I had to forget.

Quickly wiping away my tears, I pulled out my phone, fumbling through my contacts until I found Angel's number, his goofy picture appearing when I hit 'call'

"Baby, I have missed you." His husky voice hit me like a steam engine, my body responding immediately. I had missed him too.

"I have missed you too, can you come over?" I asked, I needed to feel him. I just needed to feel.

"I'm already out the door…" He said in a husked whisper, I could hear him pulling his keys out of his pocket.

"Hurry, Angel." I said before cutting off the call.

Tonight I was going to make love to Angel. I was going to apologize to him through my actions. And although we have never gone that far in our relationship, I think it is time to move in that direction. Logan and I will never be, so I needed to move on. I needed a distraction from my thoughts of him and that distraction was Angel.

I decided to unpack my clothes while I waited for Angel to show up. I hated unpacking, but I thought it best to get it over with. But when I opened up my case, my eyes locked on my father's letter and guitar pick, my heart slamming to the front of my chest. As I ran my fingers along the crisp envelope, the sound of his song floated through my mind as I hummed to the tune. Closing my eyes, I let the song drift through me in my mind, absorbing the pained love in the song.

Seconds...

Minutes...

Hours...

Time just seemed to stand still as I lived and breathed the song that meant so much to me. I didn't know how long I was stood there, trying to soak in the song. But I was suddenly pulled from the memories when I heard a knock at my door, Angel.

I quickly made my way to the door, butterflies raging in the pit of my stomach as it became acutely aware of what I was just about to do. I inhaled slowly as I tried to steady my breathing when I opened the door, gasping as two beautiful blue eyes locked with mine. Moments passed, not one of us moving for the other. Our eyes locked in an embrace like I have never felt, fire and ice blended together within my body, warming me before pulling my temperature down to dangerous levels, levels that only Angel could bring me to in a heartbeat and without a moment's notice. Suddenly he flipped the switch, turning on the warm light at the center of my core.

My desire welled and strained, begging me to fuel it, release it and roll in it. Before I even knew what I was doing, I flung my body straight into the strong arms in front of me, pressing my lips to Angel's. I ran my tongue along the seam of his bottom lip, begging for entry. The groan that released from his throat instantly sent tingles throughout my body, the sinful taste of him washed over me as I was lifted from the ground. With my legs wrapped around his waist and his hands on my ass, he devoured me with his mouth, sucking, licking, stroking my body into a frenzy of tangled guilt and desire.

"Fuck I have missed you. Your taste is intoxicating. So fucking sweet." Angel growled against my lips. He was pushing me further down a road, a road I didn't want to come back from.

We were suddenly moving, Angel walked as he stroked my tongue as if searching for something, the taste of coffee hit my taste buds as he took my tongue between his lips, sucking soft and slow. Pulling a moan from my lips, I needed him now.

"Angel..." I moaned. "Please, don't stop."

Sensing what I was referring to, Angel placed me gently on the bed before crawling up my body, slowly and seductively. This man would be my undoing. His beautiful blue eyes bore straight through me as he steadied himself above me. His arms either side of my head, holding his weight from my body.

"Are you sure about this?" He asked, leaning into my neck and peppering my skin with sweet, slow kisses.

"Oh, God yes." I panted back as he took my earlobe between his teeth, nibbling gently.

"Then you are wearing too many clothes, baby." He whispered huskily into my ear.

The sheer black blouse I was wearing was soon ripped from my body. Buttons scattered across the room, bouncing from the walls only to silence as they fell to the wooden floor. My black lace bra now exposed to Angel's beautiful eyes as he took in my creamy skin. He ran his fingertips over my rib cage, pulling shivers from my body with the gentlest of touches.

Before I could feel self-conscious from baring my body to him, my eyes went wide as Angel bowed his head and ran his tongue across each one of my ribs. Once he was finished tracing the lines on one side of my body, he swiftly moved to the next, sending my mind spiraling.

"Your skin is even sweeter than those lips of yours. Now I am dying to know what this tastes like." He hummed against my skin while tracing a line over the seam of my jeans between my legs, pulling an approving moan from my lips.

The moan was enough for him to push us further as my jeans were suddenly no longer on my legs, they were now on the floor alongside my ripped blouse. I was now only in my black lace bra and panties. Angel's eyes raked over my body as he sat back, drinking me in.

"What are you thinking?" I asked tentatively, Angel hadn't muttered a word since discarding my jeans. He was completely silent as his eyes took in my body that lay beneath him.

"I'm thinking that my dreams didn't do your body justice, Neva, fuck you're beautiful." He said as he traced the line of my panties at my hip, my desire welling, silently begging him to take them from my body.

As if Angel was reading my mind, I heard the unmistakable sound of fabric ripping. I gasped as I watched a sinful smirk pull at his lips. Frozen with desire as my panties disappeared into the back pocket of his jeans, I was turned on beyond belief knowing he had my ripped panties so close to his damn body.

"I'm only going to ask this one more time baby, because I don't think I could stop once I have a taste." His eyes locked with mine before teasing my mouth with his tongue. "Are. You. Sure?"

My mind couldn't form words, the knot in my stomach became more intense with every passing minute. Nodding, I silently answered his question. Groaning at my response, he quickly lowered his lips to my core, placing the tenderest of kisses between my slick folds.

"You have no idea how fucking addictive your taste is, Neva, no fucking idea." He growled, as the intense onslaught of his tongue teased me into a place I couldn't even begin to understand. As Angel intensified the pressure of his tongue, my body hummed in response. My hands flew into his silky hair, taking it between my fingers as I tugged and pulled him closer to my body. He consumed me.

"Angel…" I moaned, his name swiftly dying on my lips when he took my clit between his teeth and bit down, hard. He quickly soothed the sting with a sudden flick of his tongue, it was enough for the dam to burst and throw me over the edge, plunging me into complete and utter ecstasy.

My body purred and glowed as I came down from such an intense orgasm that I almost hadn't noticed Angel had stripped his body of clothing. He wore only a pair of tight black boxers that did nothing to hide his hardness. I watched as he crawled up my body, trailing light kisses from my hip to my stomach, grazing his teeth across my navel before moving up and landing on the swell of my breasts. Skillfully he swiftly unclasped my bra and removed it from my body, taking my right breast in his hand and rolling my hard peak between his thumb and finger while pulling the other into his mouth.

"I am going to worship your body, Neva. You aren't going to be able to sit down without thinking of me, thinking of us." He said against my breast. "Moan once if you understand." He demanded as he pinched my hard peak in between his fingertips, pulling a moan from my mouth.

"Good girl." He chuckled, the sound of his laugh turning me on so much more.

"Angel, I need you." I groaned, suddenly becoming more confident. But on the inside I was a quivering wreck, I needed Angel to erase the memory of Logan, of all the guilt I felt. I needed him.

"I know baby."

Taking his hands away from my body I could hear the telltale sound of a condom wrapper ripping, his mouth was still torturing my body with every flick of his tongue against my peak, sending jolts of electricity to pierce through my body. His tongue continued its onslaught against my nipple when I felt the tip of Angel's hardness against my opening.

"Angel, please." I was begging him to take me, but he was teasing me and he knew it. I was so fired up that not having Angel inside me wasn't an option. I took him by surprise, pushing back against his hardness, causing him to plunge inside me so fast I felt dizzy with lust.

"Ah, Christ Neva." He panted as he stilled inside me. "Are you trying to kill me?" He asked with his eyebrow raised.

I couldn't think of a witty come back, nor did I want to, I needed him to move.

Pushing myself up on my elbows, I watched as Angel looked

down between us, right where we were joined as one. Catching him off guard I wrapped my hand around his neck and pulled him back down to the bed with me.

"Fuck me, Angel."

"Fuck." He growled before his tongue probed my mouth, mirroring what he was doing to my core. Plunging deep inside me, he pulled the most carnal moans from my mouth.

This wasn't sweet or tender love making. This was rip your panties off, scream-your-name fucking. And I loved it.

A familiar knot was forming somewhere deep inside of me once again as he filled me to the hilt. Stars danced in front of my eyes as sinful groans escaped Angel's lips. As the knot got tighter, I was suddenly thrown back to the night with Logan. The way he felt inside me, the way he made me feel while inside me. My body screamed yes while my head said no. I shouldn't be doing this with Angel. I should be telling him what I did. All I could see, all I could feel was Logan, until Angel suddenly angled his hips, tearing a scream from my body as my orgasm ripped straight through me, cutting me in half.

With two more angled strokes that kept my orgasm spiraling, Angel came with a deep growl, his fingers tightening around my hips before dropping his weight on top of me.

That night after Angel left to go home, I silently shed two tears, one for the I man have broken beyond repair, and one for the man who I didn't deserve.

## twenty-four

I BUMPED INTO LOGAN FOR THE first time just a week after we had slept together, and when I say bumped, I mean it literally. I walked straight into his hard chest, not looking where I was going. Awkward would be putting it mildly. Logan looked like shit, his hair was no longer mussed and sexy, and it looked like it needed a good wash. His eyes were lined with dark circles and bloodshot, he looked how I felt.

It seemed as though fate was constantly fucking me over from the mistake I made with Logan, but it wasn't a mistake, was it? I loved every minute of it until the guilt consumed me, the realization that Logan and I couldn't be together was hard enough to swallow without the guilt dangling down the back of my throat as well.

Fate seemed to be reveling in my silent misery as I saw Logan at every turn. Every time our eyes locked, he would offer me a smirk, clearly enjoying watching me squirm as if seeking revenge.

But I deserved it, I fucked him over, so fate was doing the same.

My relationship with Logan was strained to say the least, and people were noticing that we were no longer the happy duo anymore. Even Tate was becoming suspicious, which freaked me the hell out. Low was staying out of it. One night she confessed that she couldn't be a part of it. If Tate ever found out, then she would deny any and all knowledge of it. Drunk or not, I believed every word.

Now college life was becoming difficult as I tried to avoid Logan at every turn, but somehow he was always within my line of sight. Sometimes he would stand there with his hands in his pockets with a smirk on his face, others he would be sucking face with Georgia or some other willing participant. To say it didn't hurt would be an absolute lie.

"Logan." I gasped in shock from his appearance.

"Don't, Neva." He gritted, unable to look at me.

"Hey, baby." I felt Angel's arms wrap around my waist from behind me. My eyes went wide as I watched Logan's face fall.

"Walker." Logan looked as though he had swallowed a sour lemon as he dismissively acknowledged Angel.

"White." Angel grunted back.

The tension between the three of us was so thick you could have cut through it with a knife. I could only watch as Angel and Logan eyed each other as if sizing one another up. I needed to get Angel out of here.

"See you around, Logan." I muttered quickly before grabbing Angel by the wrist and dragging him down the corridor with me.

"Yeah, see you around, White." Angel said over his should with a smug smile, taunting Logan further.

When we finally got out of Logan's line of sight, I pushed Angel against a row of lockers that lined the wall behind him, pulling an 'oomph' from his lips.

"What the hell was that, Angel?" I spat. I can't believe he had just done that, what was his problem? I had no idea if Angel knew about what happened between Logan and I but this was making me nervous.

"He pisses me off. I won't apologize for it either. He's a fucking tool! He treats you like shit and any other female who gains his attention." He replied, the tone of his voice rising. Making me jump from the sheer boom within it.

"Angel, please just drop it." I didn't want to argue with him. If I did, I could make it worse by defending Logan. And by the look in his eyes right now, I knew it wasn't a good idea.

"I'm not making any promises I can't keep." He sighed before placing his hands on my hips, pulling me towards him. "But I'll try, for you." He said near my ear before claiming my mouth with his.

The days that followed flew by without any incident, well that was until the morning after the football game. Tate had asked Low and me to come and watch the game. Football season had just started and Low was looking forward to watching Tate in action. Me, on the other hand? Not so much. As Low and I took our seats in the bleachers, waiting for the game to start, I suddenly decided this really wasn't a good idea. Not only was Tate on the team but Logan was too. I could just about deal with seeing him briefly on campus but this was going to kill me. But before I could stand to leave, music blared from the speakers and out came the guys. Tate, Logan, Ace, Zane and Colt and the rest of the team made their way on to the field. The whistle blew only a few minutes later.

I couldn't tell you what the score was. I couldn't tell you who won, either, as my eyes were glued to Logan and his body as it rippled under his jersey. I knew I shouldn't be looking at him, but I couldn't stop. I was a moth drawn to the flame, a very hot flame at that. As the game drew to a close, I gasped as our eyes locked. But instead of the saddened face I had seen just days before, he wore a smirk...his sexy smirk. It completely knocked me off guard, my heart hammering in my chest at finally getting to see his gorgeous face again. He quickly winked in my direction before pulling off his jersey and tucking it into the waist band of his pants, revealing his tight abs. I'd run my fingers over those abs only weeks ago.

Reluctantly tearing my gaze from his body, my eyes landed on Low who, judging from the scowl on her face, noticed mine and Logan's moment. Shit!

"Come on." She said exasperated, before making her way down from the bleachers to the guys' locker room.

As we waited for Tate, it became apparent who won from the whooping and hollering coming from inside the guys' locker room. Logan seemed to have that effect on me. Whether I could control it or not, he could make me forget that there is a world outside of us. Time just seems to stop when we are together, as if nothing else mattered as long as we are together.

"Did you hear what I said, baby girl?" I was suddenly pulled out of my thoughts by Tate's question, see? He wasn't even around and I couldn't even pay attention to anything or anyone else.

"Huh? What?"

"Logan said to meet him at 'The Spot.'"

My eyes grew wide at his reply, only days ago Logan couldn't even look at me and now he wants to see me? What was going on?

"You okay, sis?" Tate asked, noticing my shocked expression.

"Yeah, fine. I'll see you guys later." I said trying to act nonchalantly.

"Call me later." Low said with a pointed look as she leaned into my brother's arms, clearly not happy with the situation.

"Okay." I muttered before walking out of the building towards 'The Spot'.

My heart hammered against my chest as if wanting to escape, my palms were wet with nerves as my legs shook uncontrollably. I didn't know if this was a reaction for Logan actually wanting me near him or just nerves for wondering what the hell this was about.

Taking the long way around through campus, I watched as other students carried on with their normal routines, not knowing that I was dealing with a battle in my head. As I neared the football field, I quickly noticed a figure leaning against the large oak tree that sat just in front of 'our' bench. I didn't have to look at the person's face to know it was Logan. His back was pressed against the tree and his right leg bent at the knee, his foot propped on the trunk of the tree. Just the way he leaned against it was enough to know it was him, the last of the evening rays of sunlight peered through the branches of the old oak tree showcasing his stunning chiseled features. I couldn't help but notice just how beautiful he truly was, he took my breath away.

"You came." Logan's voice cut through my thoughts as I stepped towards him.

He was still in his football uniform, his jersey now back on, it was tight against his muscled chest as if straining to escape. My eyes traveled to his gorgeous face, and I think I moaned slightly at the sight of him in a snap back cap that he was wearing backwards, he looked edible. As I raked my eyes over his body, I noticed him smirk. Shit, he had seen me checking him out.

"What's this about, Logan?" I asked nervously, trying to wipe the smug smile off of his face.

"Look I..." Logan started, pulling his cap off of his head and running his fingers through his hair. "I have tried to do as you asked. I tried to get you out of my damn head but...I can't, nor do I want to. You hurt me, Neva, like nobody else could. But I can't carry on without you. Without us...I miss us." He finished on a whisper before placing his cap back on his head.

My mom once said, we hurt the people we love the most, but the ability for them to love you despite the hurt is special and the most beautiful gift, it's the gift of forgiveness. I never really understood the word forgiveness until that day. Logan was willing to forgive me for what I had done to him, but I knew that he would never forget.

"Logan, we can't do this."

"Neva, I'm asking to be your friend, not your mistress. Wait, what's the male version of a mistress? Mister?" He asked, becoming more confused the more he thought about it, making me chuckle.

"Just friends?" I asked, bringing his attention back to the original conversation.

"Just friends." He repeated.

"Okay, but Logan, if we do this then there needs to be some rules." I said, I didn't want this becoming an even bigger mess than it already was.

"Okay...." He replied, drawing the word out.

"No touching, kissing, flirting, no teasing Angel, and definitely no referring to that night." I ended in a blush as I remembered exactly what happened that night.

"No touching, huh?" He asked before pushing back from the tree, stepping towards me. "Not at all?" He asked as he leaned in close enough to feel the heat of his breath against my skin, but not close enough to touch me.

Breathless, I nodded my head to his question.

"Okay, I can live with that." He said quickly before moving away from my body, causing me to breathe quickly to stop my erratic heart from bursting from my chest.

"Good." I said with a tight smile. "I need to go. I said I would meet Low to study."

The sudden urge to kiss Logan's full lips was so strong. It hit me at full force, so I lied. Just being around Logan did things to my body I couldn't control, and right now I needed that control.

"Okay, I'll see you tomorrow?"

"Sure." I said as I started walking towards the dorms. "Lover." I shouted over my shoulder quickly, chuckling at Logan's confused face.

"Huh?"

"A male mistress is called a lover." I said as I broke out into giggles. God he was cute when he looked confused.

Ah, shut up, Neva!

## twenty-five

OVER THE NEXT COUPLE OF days, things went back to normal, well whatever 'normal' was. My days were crammed with exams, assignments and figuring Angel out. Something was off, if I asked Angel to come over there always seemed to be an excuse that he couldn't make it and when I did see him he wasn't himself. He was edgy, skittish, and usually in a bad mood.

The day Angel snapped was a Thursday. I had received a text from him telling me he would be over in ten minutes. Pulling out my lyrics for a song I was working on. I decided to work on it as I waited for him to show up.

Four hours passed...He didn't show up.

It was 3:00 am when I finally got a call from him. To say I was unhappy was an understatement and what made it worse was that he was drunk, absolutely wasted.

"Baby, I'm soooo sorry! Some friends came over with some beers and I forgot the time." He slurred. I wouldn't normally have minded, but I had no idea who his friends were, seeing as he hadn't introduced me to any. He seemed to prefer his own company.

"Could you maybe next time text me to let me know? It's 3:00 am, Angel!" I said, becoming more frustrated with all the noise in the background. It sounded more like he was in a bar than at his house.

"You're not my fucking keeper, Neva!" Angel spat, completely taking me by surprise.

But before I could respond, the line went dead, wow!

Sleep didn't come easily that night as my mind went into overdrive. I wondered what the hell was going on with Angel and why had he gone off like that? Was he really with his friends? I had only met one of his friends, and that was Dex. Was he seeing someone else? Ugh, I was such a hypocrite.

The next morning, Angel couldn't have been any more apologetic. He wrapped his arms around my waist as soon as I opened my dorm room door, begging me to forgive him.

"Baby, I'm so sorry about last night, some of the guys turned up from Bones." He sighed as he placed his face into the crook of my neck, gently placing his lips against my skin beneath the shell of my ear. "I drank a little too much and...I'm so sorry for shouting at you like that, baby."

His voice vibrated against my neck as he lay feather-light kisses, his touch dancing across my skin. I felt his tongue dart out, tasting the saltiness of my skin as he slowly ran it over the sensitive spot at the hollow of my neck.

"I forgive you." Why was I mad at him again? I ran my hands through his beautifully thick dark hair, scratching his scalp before pulling his hair with a tug, bringing his face eye level with mine.

"Just don't do it again." I said before quickly pulling his lips to mine, a groan escaping his lips as our lips met. The hint of last night's Jack Daniels and fresh mint toothpaste hit me as he slowly ran his tongue over my bottom lip, it was a dangerous cocktail and I was addicted.

Angel's tongue slowly sought mine. Both his hands gently cradled my face. His lips were so soft against my own, taking me completely by surprise. Angel had never kissed me like this, so soft and slow. Our relationship was built on intense heat and desire but this was different, this was...this was slow and deliberate. Making me rethink everything I ever knew about Angel, everything I felt for him.

"The thought of being without you kills me. I need you, Neva, I need...us." He said gently against my lips, the whisper of his voice vibrated straight through to my core.

"I need you too." I said without hesitation, before crashing my lips to his, pulling a deep and carnal groan from his lips. His tongue quickly found mine once again, exploring my mouth with sheer determination as if searching for the lost treasure in the deepest seas. The strokes of his tongue against mine were as soft as pure silk, his hands sliding down to my waist before settling on my ass.

"I am going to show you just how much I need you, just how much you need me. I won't finish until I have you screaming my name." Angel promised against my mouth, lifting me up off of the ground as I wrapped my legs around his waist.

Walking towards my bed, Angel slowly lowered me down, feeling the soft sheets against my back. A whimper quickly escaped my lips as Angel crawled up my body, his left knee pressed tight against my core.

"I've fallen, Neva." Angel whispered against my skin, nuzzling his nose into my neck. My breathing turning into hard pants as I took in what Angel was saying. "I've fallen hard. I want you to fall with me. Fall with me, Neva...Let me show you just how much I need you, how much you need me. How much I..." He quickly closed his eyes tight, as if mustering the courage he needed from deep within him. I watched in anticipation as he slowly opened his eyes, I suddenly gasped as I noticed his eyes had glossed over, the emotion evident as his deep blue eyes turned a few shades darker. "How desperate I am for you, you are the music to my soul, Neva, you brought me back to life again. The word 'love' doesn't even come close to what I feel for you. I need you and right now...I need you to need me too."

"My fallen Angel, I need you too...Desperately."

Before I could even react, Angel's lips crashed against mine. The deliciousness of his unique taste pushed my mind towards the edge, teetering so close to the cliff. Damn, I was ready to jump.

"Angel." I moaned against his lips, knowing just a whisper of his name was enough to send him crazy.

"Neva, I need you. Now." He growled, hitching my right leg around his waist before taking the kiss deeper. I moaned when Angel's tongue teased my bottom lip, desperately seeking entry. "Baby, let me make love to you." He pleaded, peppering my neck with slow and deliberate kisses, splintering my mind in half. Angel consumes me, his kisses scorch me, his touch brands me... like nothing else.

"Yes, Angel." I moaned, walking backwards towards my bed. Angel was undoing me, making me his. He could make me forget my own damn name in a single heartbeat.

His hands quickly grasped my waist, guiding me further up the bed, his eyes never leaving mine as he crawled up the bed with me. His penetrating gaze marking me with every fleeting second, I needed him...more than he would ever know.

The tank top and boy shorts that were once secured to my body were now on the floor in a crumpled heap. I was once again naked under Angel's body. Watching as he slowly took in my body, his fingertips slowly running up the center of my stomach, leaving behind a wake of goose bumps.

"Jesus, Neva." He whispered, locking his gaze with my own before swiftly removing his shirt and jeans. "You're so damn beautiful." He threw the last of his clothing on the floor alongside mine.

I gasped, which was followed quickly by a moan as Angel's finger slowly slid in between my wet folds, making my head swim with unfaltering pleasure. Biting my lip, I watched as Angel ran his fingers through my warmth, taking in every single hard ridge of his defined body. He was amazingly beautiful, and he was all mine.

"Angel...please." I begged, I needed him and I didn't want to wait another minute.

"What do you need, Neva? Tell me." He asked, lowering his lips to my neck, teasing me as his tongue gently probed my skin.

"I...I, oh God." I moaned, my brain-to-mouth filter was becoming tangled as Angel gently nipped my neck while his fingers explored my sex, gliding with ease.

"Tell me want you need, Neva." He repeated, carrying on the onslaught of all but teasing me into a coma with one hand, while pulling out a condom and taking it between his teeth. Ripping open the packet, I watched as he rolled the condom over his length, pleasure clouding my vision when I suddenly felt his hardness against my opening. "Tell me, Neva." He repeated as he held his lips inches away from mine, knowingly pushing me to the edge.

"I...I want you to make love to me Angel."

"Fuck..." He growled against my lips before grazing his lips against mine, his hardness slowly pushing into my entrance as his tongue met mine. My back arched as Angel pushed in to the hilt, filling me until I saw stars.

"Oh God." I moaned as Angel slowly started to move, so fucking slowly that I thought I may tumble from the cliff he had placed me on. I didn't know if I could keep at the pace Angel was setting, I was becoming delirious with need and want as he moaned against my lips.

"Angel, please...harder."

That was all it took, suddenly my wrists were pinned above my head in one hand while the other was on my hip, his fingers dug into my skin as he quickened his pace, using my wrists as leverage to plow into me.

"Neva, I need you." Angel whispered as his breathing became erratic, matching mine. Need was now so much more than a word thrown around by people from day to day, it was an urgent want, an all-consuming level of love. And I needed him too.

"Oh God, Angel. I need you too, I love you." The words were hanging in the air above me, as if I could reach out and touch them.

"Ah, shit. I love you, Neva." Angel growled as his pace was becoming staggered, shifting quickly to change the angle as he pressed against my sweet spot. I was so close to the edge, I could almost taste it. "I need you with me, Neva." He begged.

"Take me with you, Angel." I cried as an orgasm so intense jolted through my body, hurtling my body over the edge of the cliff, plunging into the watery depth below, holding onto Angel as I pulled him down with me.

"Holy. Fucking. Shit. Ah, Neva." Angel moaned as his orgasm punched him full force, his body shaking and stuttering, prolonging my own orgasm with his jerky movements.

My head spun as we both came down from our earth-shattering orgasms, our panting breaths mingling, unashamed. As Angel rested his head on my chest, our hearts lined up, so close and so soothing that I quickly fell into a blissful deep sleep.

# twenty-six

IN THE DAYS THAT PASSED, Angel was spending more time with his mom. I didn't mind, he loved his mom and from what I could gather she had been through a lot over the years.

Logan and I had been hanging out a lot more during the day since we decided to keep our relationship as friends, most of it spent studying at my place and today was no exception. Logan and I had been discussing the latest gossip from one of Ace's house parties, laughing that Ace had gotten so wasted that he ripped off all of his clothes and ran through the house, naked. We were laughing so hard when we watched the video go live on YouTube, and laughing even harder when it hit 250,000 hits.

"He is never going to live that down." Logan said chuckling, our cries of laughter slowly dying down.

"Poor Ace, but he did say that he was the sexiest guy on campus. I just can't believe he decided to prove it by running through his house naked! The image of Ace's 'hidden' piercing will be forever burned in my memory, gross." I said chuckling. The poor guy really was never going to live this down, especially from the guys on the football team.

"Do you think Ace is the sexiest guy on campus?" Logan asked with a wicked grin on his face.

"That is gross, Logan. No, I don't think he is the sexiest guy on campus. He's the most revolting!" I laughed, Ace was a great guy but he was definitely not my type.

"So who is then?" He said, wiggling his eyebrows as if insinuating that he was the sexiest, oh here we go!

"Professor Gregg Harper...there is something about -" I didn't even get a chance to even finish the sentence before Logan was tickling the shit out of me, taking me completely by surprise.

"Oh. My. God! Logan, stop. Please stop!" I yelled, laughter pouring from my mouth as he kept up the onslaught of tickling me, if he wasn't careful he was going to tickle me into a coma.

"Say it." He chuckled as he tickled me under my ribs, straddling my hips and pinning me to the bed. I knew what he wanted me to say, but I was not going to give in.

"No, never!" I said laughing so hard that I snorted like a pig, lovely!

"I won't stop until you say it, Neva!" He said with a cocky smile, finding the most sensitive spot around my waist, tickling me furiously.

"Okay, okay Logan White is the sexiest guy on campus." I said chuckling as he finally let up, before dropping his weight on top of me, taking me completely by surprise.

His lips were resting against my neck as his breath felt hot against my skin, my body flushing from the weight of him against me. Pulling back, he stroked a single piece of hair that had come loose from my sloppy bun, pushing it back behind my ear.

"You think I'm sexy?" He asked, he was so close, but I didn't have the control or power to push him from me.

"You know you're sexy, Logan, you don't need me to tell you that." I said on a shaky breath.

"Can I ask you something?" He pulled his weight from me slightly without releasing my body from under his.

"Yes." I said hoarsely.

"What did you mean when you said you were broken? Because all I see when I look at you is a heroine."

"Trust me, I'm no heroine, Logan. A heroine is a woman with courage, admired for her brave deeds. That is not me, and you know it. You have seen the nightmares."

"But that is bullshit, Neva! A heroine is a woman who comes face-to-face with heartbreak, frightening experiences, unbelievable pain or unyielding suffering and can still rebuild her life after everything and smile while doing it. You Neva, are a heroine."

Self-control? Yeah, that leaped out the window as soon as he walked through my door.

My world teetered on an unforgiving axis as I pulled Logan's lips to mine, gasping as our lips met once again, his tongue teasing my bottom lip. Letting him in, our tongues danced together as they reacquainted themselves with one another.

"I still love you, Neva." He whispered against my lips, pulling a moan from deep inside my body. With my hand in his hair, I tried to regain some control, but when Logan nibbled at my bottom lip I don't think my mind could even process what self-control meant.

"But you keep breaking my heart, at every turn." He cried before jumping off me, quickly leaving my room.

Tears slowly fell down my cheeks from Logan's admission. He still loved me and what was worse is that I loved him too but didn't have the backbone to tell him.

"Why have I just seen Logan walk out of here looking like he was about to cut a bitch?" Low said loudly as she walked through the door, slamming it shut behind her. Her brows furrowed, clearly noticing the tears that were quickly streaming down my face.

"Please don't." I said defeated, bowing my head quickly using my hair to hide my face.

"Don't...don't? Are you serious right now, Neva?" Low spat, completely taking me by surprise. "What the hell are you doing? Are you playing them both? This is not a game, Neva. You said you would choose! Now all you're doing is hurting Logan and I will not stand by and watch you do this to him." I was frozen in place, stunned by Low's outburst. She thinks I am playing a game? Is she freaking kidding me?

"I...I, shit." I stuttered, her assumption taking me by surprise. But how could I tell my best friend that I couldn't choose? How could I tell her that I loved both of them for different reasons? Angel was intense and just as broken as I was, but he was fixing me in a way I thought was impossible. I loved him because I thought I was irreversibly broken, but he was showing me that I wasn't broken...I had just gotten a little bruised on the way. Then there was Logan, who has been protecting me since I was ten, protecting me in a way that made me feel safe, feel at home. He knew me on a level that I don't think I could share with Angel. I didn't have to hide from Logan. How can I tell her that I couldn't choose just one because between them, they were both mending my broken heart?

"Have you even considered how Angel will feel when he finds out, Neva? You. Will. Break. Him." Low spat, pulling me out of my questionable thoughts as she became more and more annoyed. Her eyes never leaving mine as she quickly paced the floor in front of me. "I mean, Jesus, Neva! The guy worships the ground you walk on and all you are doing is throwing it back in his face. Stop thinking about yourself, Neva and think about the two men you are hurting over and over again."

My blood boiled at Low's words, she didn't understand. I mean, how could she? She had no idea of the daily battle I was having with my conscience and my heart, she had no idea that I had said the same things about myself over and over in my head, torturing myself day in day out. I didn't want to hurt either of them and it was never my intention, no matter how hard it was for people to grasp.

"I'm not doing this with you, Low! Seriously, back off and keep out of it. You have no idea what I go through daily and you certainly have no idea what you are talking about."

"No idea about what?"

My head quickly snapped towards the dorm door, my brother standing there looking between Low and me with a confused expression on his face.

"Nothing." I whispered, I quickly turned my gaze to Low silently pleading with her not to tell Tate what was going on.

"Tell him, Neva, or I will!" Low said quickly, totally knocking me off balance. My body buckled underneath me, knowing that I would have to tell him. Dropping to my knees, the sobs quickly tore from my throat, flinching as Tate knelt down in front of me and took me into his arms, wrapping me up in a tight hug.

"Tell me what?" Tate asked as he gently rocked me in his arms, trying to sooth me as I melted against his chest.

"I'm sorry." I said through sobs, bunching Tate's shirt in my hands trying desperately to keep him close.

"What is it, baby girl? You can tell me." He said in a soothing voice as he gently stroked my back in comfort. How do I tell my brother that I am in love with his best friend, the man who he trusted...the man that owned me like no one else could?

"I can't...I." I stuttered, the sobs coming thick and fast as my throat restricted. It was as if my body was stopping me from telling Tate the truth.

"Tell him, Neva." Low pushed, her anger seemingly toned down.

"I slept with Logan." My hand quickly flew to my mouth, stifling the gasp that was readily positioned on my lips, waiting for Tate's reaction. Waiting for him to go bat shit crazy and possibly kill Logan for betraying his trust, but...it never came.

"I know." He whispered, I quickly pulled back and stared at my brother in shock. What the hell? How could he possibly know, unless Low had told him?

"W...What are you talking about?" I said, unable to disguise the shock penetrating my voice as I looked over at Low for an answer. She shook her head, letting me know that she hadn't told him either.

"He told me, Neva." He sighed, briefly closing his eyes before slowly opening them again. "He loves you, baby girl, he has since I can remember but he is hurting. He has to watch you with Angel day in and day out and he doesn't know how long he can stay away from you, Neva, he is only so strong."

"I love him too." I admitted, my voice was so small that I wasn't sure it came from my lips. Looking up at my brother and my best friend, I realized the words had come from me, and Tate and Low had definitely heard me.

"What about Angel?" Tate added, clearly still not understanding.

"I love Angel too." I sighed, trying to find the courage to explain exactly what was going on. "I love them both, I love them for different reasons and my heart hurts every damn time I think about it. But I did choose, you guys just don't see it. I chose Angel because I love him, but I also chose him to protect Logan. I am not going to subject him to my nightmares or my past any longer. It isn't his burden to carry." The tears were coming like a tsunami, wave after wave hitting me harder and harder as I tried to explain that I was in love with two men.

"So Angel knows what happened?" Low asked as she sat down on the edge of her bed.

"No, I don't think I will ever be ready to tell him what happened. With Angel, I can just be me, not the Neva who has nightmares that scare the shit out of people who see them, not the Neva who can't get in a damn car or the Neva who can't watch news reports in case a car wreck is featured. I am so sick of being that person, I want to be me, I want to live!" My voice raised with every passing second as my anger boiled to the surface, anger towards myself and the man who claimed my father's life.

"But you are basing your relationship with Angel on a lie, he is going to find out eventually. What happens if you have a nightmare while you are with him?" Low asked tentatively.

"I won't put myself into that situation, and if it does happen, then maybe I could tell him." I threw my hands in my hair, I knew I wasn't being reasonable but why should I subject someone else to my pain. "I don't know what the hell I would do, but for right now, I don't have to tell him. For right now, I want to be normal, so will you please just respect that and stop getting on my case about it?" I spat, I just wanted them to leave the subject alone. I wasn't ready for this.

"Okay, we will drop it but what about Logan? You slept with him Neva, you can't expect him just to shut off his feelings." Tate pleaded, the concern for his friend evident in his voice.

"I don't expect him to shut off his feelings, Tate, but when I am around him, it's like my body is forcing me to stay with him and when I'm not, I am constantly thinking about him. I love him and I can't shut off my feelings for him either, but I think it would be for the best if we didn't see each other. Even as friends." The realization of what I had just said hit me hard, but I wasn't willing to show it. I can't tell Tate and Low that I wanted to be more than friends with Logan, that I wanted Logan without having to hurt Angel at the same time. Talk about a cluster fuck.

"Look, I am not going to claim that I completely understand it, but if you say you can't see Logan again, then don't. You are only going to hurt him and yourself more than you already have. Keep him at arm's length, Neva. Don't hurt him." Tate said tight lipped, squeezing my shoulders before getting up and leaving my room.

"I'm sorry, Neva but I am with your brother on this one, and you need to keep away from Logan. For everyone's sake." Low said with a tight smile before getting up and leaving the room, following my brother's footsteps.

Cluster fuck doesn't even describe what I am thinking right now...

## twenty-seven

LOOKING AT MY REFLECTION IN the mirror, I stared back at the girl I wasn't sure I knew. At the beginning of the year I wasn't sure if I could open my heart up again, now I was in a battle between trusting my head or my heart. How had my life gone down this road? I didn't know, but something was going to give soon and when it does, it was going to be one hell of a collision.

"You nearly ready, baby?" Angel shouted from outside the bathroom door.

"Yeah, just a minute." I replied, adding another coat of gloss to my lips.

Smoothing out my knee length dress, I checked my reflection once again, Angel was taking me out to dinner before going back to his place to meet his mom, I was so nervous. It had taken Low and I most of the day to decide on an outfit and after seventeen outfits were rejected, mainly by Low, we decided on a simple black dress. After smoothing out my hair, which was draped upon my shoulders in loose curls, I was ready. Taking a deep breath, I walked out of the bathroom to find Angel staring at me, wide eyed.

"Holy shit baby, you look amazing! Are you sure we can't stay here tonight? I have a really good image of you wearing nothing but those sexy black heels and draping them over my shoulders, so I can devour you." He said with a smirk, his blue eyes smoldering.

"No, we aren't skipping dinner or visiting your mom, so put your tongue back in your mouth. Come on or we'll be late." I said with a chuckle as Angel sighed dramatically.

Dinner was amazing. Angel had taken me to a small Italian bistro in town, it was small but intimate, with large candles as centerpieces and a beautiful band playing a mixture of sweet and soulful music.

Our conversations were light as we talked about music, classes and our professor, laughing at Angel's impression of him dancing around the class when he got excited, pulling attention to our table.

"Tell me about your mom." I asked as I finished a piece of garlic bread.

"Mom is amazing. She is a hairdresser. She owns a salon on the edge of town with some exclusive clientele. She loves coffee and is an amazing cook, she tried to teach me once, but I nearly burned the fucking house down." He chuckled at the memory.

There was no doubt that Angel loved his mom, just the way he spoke of her lovingly warmed my heart.

"I can't wait to meet her."

"Shit, we need to go or we are going to be late." He said, glancing at his watch.

We had walked to the restaurant. Angel didn't even bother with his car anymore, since I still couldn't get in one with anyone else other than Logan and Tate. As we rushed across town I could see Angel's shoulders tense with every step we took.

"Are you okay?" I asked, pulling on Angel's hand, stopping him mid stride.

"Yeah, I'm just nervous. I have never brought a girl home before." He said, running his hand through his hair.

"Hey, it will be fine." I said, placing a light kiss on his lips, trying to reassure him, but when our lips locked, what only intended to be an innocent kiss turned into something much more. Pulling me flush against his body, I moaned into his mouth as he ran his tongue along my bottom lip. I wrapped my arms around his neck and he swiftly deepened the kiss, exploring my mouth with his tongue. As quickly as it had started, it had finished.

"Come on, baby." Angel said with a sexy smile.

We approached a modest two-story house only ten minutes later. It was a beautiful home, made from brick. It was painted an off-white, sporting a modest garden in the front. A porch wrapped around the house, showing off large windows that were lined with beautiful flower pots.

Walking across the driveway, I spotted Angel's Mustang, still sleek and sexy just like the first day I saw it.

"Hey, sweet boy." I turned quickly to find Angel's mom standing on the porch with a loving smile on her face.

"Hey, mom." Angel replied as he released my hand from his

grasp, jogging over to his mom and giving her a tight squeeze before looking back in my direction. "Mom, this is Neva, Neva this is my mom, Vivian." Angel said, introducing us.

Vivian Walker was not what I had expected, she was stunning and completely the opposite of Angel. Her hair was a brilliant blonde, which was pinned back into a smooth chignon, her eyes a deep shade of brown and her makeup was flawless. She was certainly eye-catching.

"Call me Viv, honey." Vivian replied with a wink, flashing a set of perfect pearly whites. "Come on inside, I have made some coffee." Christ, I can't smell coffee without thoughts of Angel flashing through my mind, this could be interesting.

Stepping into the house I felt as though I had just landed into a family photo album. Pictures of Angel as a child lined the walls from being a newborn right up until the man he was today.

"Your mom loves embarrassing you too, huh?" I said as I tipped my head into the direction of a picture of him naked in the bath as a baby.

"Oh, God." He replied, chuckling before leading me into the living room, Viv was already pouring coffee into the three mugs that were on the coffee table.

"So what are you studying in college, Neva?" Viv asked as she passed Angel our coffees.

"Music, I want to be a music teacher." I replied tentatively.

"Ah, the key to my boys heart."

"Mom!" Angel cut her off and rolled his eyes.

"What, it's no secret! He loves singing in the shower too." She said with a small chuckle.

"You sing in the shower?" I asked, trying hard not to laugh

but the smell of coffee and thought of Angel in the shower quickly stopped me from laughing.

Angel groaned, rolling his eyes before sighing.

"I'm pleading the fifth!"

For the next hour Viv spoke about what Angel was like growing up, while Angel groaned with every story, causing me to laugh even harder. I couldn't wipe the smile from my face as I watched them both banter with each other, their relationship was beautiful to watch and it was clear that they were extremely close.

"Can I use your restroom?" I whispered to Angel, all the coffee Viv was supplying me with was going to make my bladder explode.

"Sure, up the stairs, first door on your left." Angel replied.

"Thanks." I said, making my way up to the first floor of the house.

But just as I was about to walk through the bathroom door, I heard a loud bang followed by a booming voice.

"There had better be some fucking beers in that refrigerator, Viv!"

Who the hell was that? Forgetting about my urgent need to pee, I started making my way down the stairs, watching as Angel and Viv came out of the living room and into the hallway. Viv's face was a picture of shock whereas Angel looked like he wasn't even fazed by this man's intrusion.

"Oh shit." I heard Viv gasp before moving quickly behind Angel.

I darted my gaze over to the doorway, my eyes locking on the source of the voice. He must have been around 6 foot, broad shoulders were attached to a muscular neck, scattered with tattoos. I didn't want to look up any further, I had seen enough to know I should fear him. But I did, my eyes suddenly locked with a set of steel blue eyes that were laced with a scattering of gold flecks, I gasped as my legs started to quiver, my heart pounding and my lungs straining for every breath.

"Well, well, well who do we have here?" The man's voice was raspy and hoarse as he slurred his words, swaying slightly as he took a gulp of beer from a bottle before throwing it against the wall. Glass shattered into tiny pieces, scattering across the hallway carpet, causing my heart to jump into my throat at the sound as I moved to stand by Angel, my hands quivering in fear.

"Who's your pet, Angel?" He snarled, his eyes wide with fury, baring the same resemblance as Angel's, but more luminous, hard and much more scary. Was this man Angel's father?

"Well?" His voice boomed across the narrow hallway, making me flinch. But it wasn't his voice that was scaring the shit out of me, it was his eyes, it was as if they were throwing daggers right through me.

"This is Neva James, my girlfriend." Angel said tight-lipped, his posture becoming hard and tense.

"Where the fuck are your manners, boy?" He spat, stepping towards Angel but before I knew what was happening I heard the loud crack of bones crushing as the man swiftly ploughed his fist into Angel's jaw. "Introduce us!"

I gasped at the contact, Angel not even flinching at this man's attack, my fear rooting me to the ground. I wanted to comfort him but I was rendered motionless.

"Neva, this is my father, Jack Walker." Angel grunted, trying to push through the pain in his jaw. Oh shit, this was his dad.

"They call me The Jackal." He slurred, quickly turning to Angel. "She looks fucking delicious."

Angel didn't move one single inch as his dad licked his lips, turning my stomach.

"It's a damn shame that I have to ruin those pretty good looks of yours, otherwise I would have loved a taste. I bet you taste fucking sweet, does she taste sweet, boy?"

My heart slammed to the front of my chest as my eyes darted to Angel, who still hadn't moved or said a word without indication from his father. What the hell was going on? What the fuck was he talking about? I didn't even know this man and he was threatening to hurt me? But I couldn't question or protest as my throat became dry and my tongue became heavy in my mouth.

"Neva, come here baby." Angel whispered. But I couldn't move, my feet were attached firmly to the ground. "Neva!" Angel whisper-shouted, gaining my attention I turned, my eyes locking with his. The blue pools that so often mesmerized me with the depth of color, now made my skin crawl from the uncanny resemblance they held to his father's.

"I...I...what is going on Angel?" I stuttered, trying to keep my eyes on the man who had claimed me. I couldn't get the image of Angel's father's words out of my mind, he wanted to hurt me and I had no fucking idea why. I had only met him today, and Angel had never really spoken about his father before. But looking at Angel, I watched as he averted his eye from me, looking at the ground nervously. It was a side of Angel I never thought I would see; vulnerable, scared and maybe a hint of guilt?

"I'm sorry. I never wanted this to happen. I need you to believe me when I tell you just how much you mean to me. How much I love you. How much I need you." Angel said, a gasp escaped me as I watched a single tear roll down his beautiful face. Now I was freaking out, what the hell is going on?

"What is going on Angel? You're scaring me."

"My deepest regret was finding you, but loving you is my every need. Maybe one day you will understand and maybe even...maybe even forgive me."

Angel's hand rested on my shoulder and squeezed lightly, I didn't understand. What was he saying? Maybe one day I will understand? I have no idea what the hell I am supposed to even try and understand! My head was swimming with questions that I just couldn't seem to ask, I didn't even know if I wanted to ask.

"Well, fuck me. You were only supposed to find her, not fall in love with her. You fucking idiot, can you do a single think right? Fuck, you're just like your bastard of a mother." Jack's eyes darted to Viv's cowering frame, who was still shielding herself behind her son. "After ten fucking years you are just going to hide behind this little fucking runt? You're not even going to greet your husband with a kiss?" He slurred.

"That's enough!" I spat, all eyes darted to me shocked by my sudden outburst. I didn't even realize it had escaped my lips until I saw the venom pouring from Jack's eyes. "What the hell is going on?" I seethed.

"You were brought here for a reason. It wasn't coincidence that you and Angel were to stumble into each other's lives. I. Made. It. Happen." He chuckled, clearly laughing at his own twisted and sick joke. A smug smile crept across his disgusting face before he continued. "In loving memory of Brandon James, husband to Lorena James, father to Tate and Neva James. Gone but never forgotten." I gasped as he recited the newspaper article about my father's death, what the fuck?

"How did you know my father?" I asked timidly, my voice breaking from the dryness in my throat.

"How did I know him? How the fuck did I know him?" He spat as he paced back and forth on the spot, throwing his fingers through his matted hair before walking towards me calmly. His face broke into a disgusting smile, baring his yellowing teeth.

"Your bastard father was the one who put me in fucking jail for ten years." He said calmly.

His words suddenly hit me like a freight train, derailing me completely. The man standing in front of me was the man who had killed my father, the man who took away my daddy.

"You fucking disgust me." The words few from my mouth so quickly I didn't even know if it was actually me who had said them, lost in the haze of fear and fury I didn't even notice that Jack had moved out of my face. I also didn't register Jack's fist moving swiftly towards my face until I heard Angel finally open his mouth.

"NO!"

Car crash.

Drunk driver.

Revived at the scene.

I will always protect you from your demons Neva.

I need you.

My past will tear us apart, don't you see that?

Maybe one day you will understand.

Ten white petals.

One yellow center...

With my eyes closed and my heart heavy, I finally let go.

Finally, letting the darkness consume me.

The End

*acknowledgements*

To my readers who have been with me since the beginning, thank you. I couldn't do what I do without you. Your love for my characters is what keeps me writing.

Thank you to my amazing editor, Emma Mack of Ultra Editing Co, without whom I would probably be in a white padded cell.

To my super hero agent, Kimberly Brower of Rebecca Friedman Literary Agency, there have been so many times that you've pulled me back from the writing edge. I'm forever in your debt.

Huge thank you to my amazing formatter, Cassandra Roop of Pink Ink Designs, you've made *all* of my pages come to life.

Thank you to my amazing family and friends for standing by me when things got tough, and supported me through it, no matter what.

For my Heartbreakers, thank you for supporting me. Your belief and support mean the absolute world. Thank you for being such an open and loving group of people.

Finally, a special shout-out to the bloggers, if it wasn't for your constant enthusiasm, I would still be staring at a blank page.

# about the author

S.K. Hartley is a wife and mother to an oil soaked husband and a tomato sauce covered son by day, by night an International Bestselling Author whose first novel, Finding You, quickly shot up the charts in fall 2013.

Since releasing her first novel, she then went on to release two more books in the series, Finding Me & Finding Us, proving that New Adult is vastly popular among readers and writers a like.

Located in the not so sunny North West of England, UK, S.K. Hartley deals with daily battles against her love of chocolate, coffee addiction, defying autocorrect and her weird obsession with Pinterest and Instagram.

## Follow S.K. Hartley!

www.facebook.com/RestrainedLove
www.twiter.com/S_K_Hartley
www.skhartleyauthor.com
www.goodreads.com/author/show/7020553.S_K_Hartley